Bridesmaid for Hire

—

Marie Ferrarella

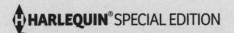
HARLEQUIN SPECIAL EDITION

Recycling programs
for this product may
not exist in your area.

ISBN-13: 978-1-335-57414-5

Bridesmaid for Hire

Copyright © 2019 by Marie Rydzynski-Ferrarella

This edition published by arrangement with Harlequin Books S.A.

For questions and comments about the quality of this book, please contact us at CustomerService@Harlequin.com.

® and TM are trademarks of Harlequin Enterprises Limited or its corporate affiliates. Trademarks indicated with ® are registered in the United States Patent and Trademark Office, the Canadian Intellectual Property Office and in other countries.

Printed in U.S.A.

USA TODAY bestselling and RITA® Award–winning author **Marie Ferrarella** has written more than two hundred and fifty books for Harlequin, some under the name Marie Nicole. Her romances are beloved by fans worldwide. Visit her website, marieferrarella.com.

To
Ellie Melgar,
Not Even Four Years Old Yet
And Already
An Endless Source Of
Inspiration
To Me.

Prologue

"You understand that I normally don't like to interfere in my children's lives," Anna Bongino stated emphatically.

Animated, the silver-haired, well-dressed woman was perched on the edge of her chair in Maizie Sommers's real estate office. Anna drew ever closer to the edge as she spoke.

Despite the declaration written in bold black letters on the outer door, the subject under discussion was definitely *not* about real estate.

"You're a mother, Anna," Maizie told the woman in the kind, understanding voice she often used when calming down nervous first-time buyers. "Interfering in our children's lives is written in the bylaws. You'll find it listed right after toilet training and staying up all night."

Sitting back in her chair, Maizie smiled at her friend.

She might have been in charge of a thriving real estate business that she'd started right after losing her husband, but the subject matter under discussion was just as near and dear to her heart. Maybe even more so. To her, matchmaking wasn't just a hobby. Maizie felt it was her calling.

When approached for help, she and her lifelong best friends, Celia Parnell and Theresa Manetti, both successful small business owners in their own right, pooled their vast clientele and were able to hone in on just the right match. So far, they were batting a thousand.

Finding the perfect match had all begun innocently enough. They had decided to take matters into their own hands and find matches for their own children. That successful endeavor had slowly blossomed to the point that their services were sought out by desperate parents or relatives who wanted only the best for their loved ones. They wanted them to have a chance at the happiness that had, heretofore, been eluding them.

Which was why Anna Bongino was now sitting in her office, tripping over her own tongue and trying not to be overly embarrassed as she stated what had brought her here today.

"Gina is a bright, outgoing, beautiful girl," Anna said almost insistently.

"I've seen her photograph," Maizie replied, agreeing, at least for now, with the "beautiful" part of Anna's assessment.

"But she's turning thirty-two soon," Anna practically wailed.

"That's not exactly having one foot in the grave yet, Anna," Maizie pointed out, doing her best to maintain a serious expression. This "advanced" age was clearly a sore point for Anna.

"Well, it might as well be," Anna cried. She drew herself up. "Did I tell you what my unmarried daughter does for a living?"

"No, we haven't gotten to that information yet," Maizie replied.

"She's a professional bridesmaid," Anna all but cried. "Have you ever heard of such a thing? I certainly haven't," Anna declared distastefully, then sighed mightily. "You know that old saying, always a bridesmaid, never a bride?"

"I am familiar with it," Maizie answered sympathetically.

"Well, Gina's taken it to a new level. Professional bridesmaid," she said with disdain. "She made the whole thing up." It was obvious that Anna was not giving her daughter any points for creativity as she went on complaining. "It's Gina's job to make sure that the bride experiences her day without any drama. Gina makes sure to handle any and all emergencies on the 'big' day so that the bride and her bridesmaids don't have to endure any of the hassle."

"That's rather a unique vocation," Maizie commented. "What was Gina before she became this 'professional bridesmaid?'" she asked, as calm as Anna was agitated. Maizie was trying to get to know her subject so that she and her friends could ultimately find the young woman's match.

It seemed clear that she had brought up a sore point. Anna's face fell as she responded, "Gina was an accountant with a Fortune 500 company. She was going places, Maizie. But she said it wasn't 'fulfilling enough' for her.

So she gave all that up to help brides have a wonderful day—as if becoming a bride wasn't wonderful enough."

"Is that why she gave up accounting?" Maizie asked, trying to get as complete and rounded a picture of the young woman as possible. "Because it wasn't fulfilling enough for her?"

Anna huffed. "That's what she said. It also wasn't 'hands on' enough for her. Gina had been a bridesmaid so many times—six," Anna emphasized almost grudgingly, "that she felt she could take this so-called 'knowledge' and parlay it into this 'creative' vocation." Anna shook her head in complete despair.

"Now she's so busy getting other people married off that she doesn't have any time to look around for a suitable man herself." Almost completely off her seat by now, Anna leaned forward over Maizie's desk, her hand reaching for Maizie's. "I need help, Maizie. I need you to throw a sack over my daughter's head and whisk her away to some wonderful hideaway where she can meet the man of her dreams—or barring that, anything close to it," Anna stressed.

The image amused Maizie. "And what's 'he' like, or don't you know?"

"Oh, I know. Or I thought I did. Gina was going out with Shane Callaghan about ten years ago. It looked as if that match was getting serious. I had such high hopes for it. And then, just like that, it *stopped* being serious." It pained Anna to talk about it, even after ten years. "They broke up."

"Why?"

Anna frowned, frustrated. "Damned if I know. Gina wouldn't talk about it. I suspect that she got cold feet, but because I couldn't get her to talk about it, I don't know if I'm right or not."

"Shane Callaghan," Maizie repeated. The name sounded vaguely familiar, but for the life of her, Maizie didn't know why or where she had heard it before. "Do you know where this Shane Callaghan is now?"

Anna shook her heard. "I haven't a clue. If I did, I wouldn't be here. I'd be going right up to him and doing everything I could to bring him and Gina together. According to Gina, he vanished right after college graduation."

Maizie smiled, knowing how frustrating it could be, sitting on the sidelines. That was obviously not Anna Bongino's style. "There are laws against kidnapping in this state."

Anna shrugged. "It would be worth it if it meant that Gina finally had the right man in her life."

"And you think that this Shane Callaghan is the right one?" Maizie questioned.

"Oh absolutely. I'd bet my soul on it," she declared with conviction. "So, will you help, Maizie?" Anna asked eagerly, searching Maizie's face. "Will you help my daughter find the right man and get married?"

"I can certainly try," Maizie promised the attractive woman, shaking her hand.

"'Try'?" Anna asked, a touch of disappointment in her voice.

"Only God gives guarantees, but if it helps, our track record is a hundred percent so far," Maizie assured her friend.

Anna received the news and beamed. "It helps a great deal."

Chapter One

Eight-year-old Adelyn Loren nodded her approval as she watched, mesmerized, as her aunt adjusted a light blue, floor-length bridesmaid dress. There was a touch of wonder in the little girl's soft brown eyes.

"Aunt Gina?" the little girl, known to her family as Addie, asked hesitantly.

The dark-haired little girl jumped off the bed. She had followed Gina into the room when her aunt had asked her if she wanted to see what the dress looked like on her. A fashion buff, even at the tender age of eight, the girl came in eagerly.

She finally had the dress right, Gina thought, looking herself over in her sister's full-length mirror. "What, baby?" Gina asked absently.

Encouraged, Addie's voice sounded a little more confident as she asked, "How many times do you have to do it?"

Gina turned away from the mirror. The dress her latest client had initially picked out had been dowdy and downright awful. With a little bit of subtle hinting, Gina had managed to convince the young woman that being backed up by an attractive-looking bridal party would only serve to highlight her own gown on her big day. That succeeded in making *everyone* happy.

Satisfied, Gina gave her niece her full attention. The little girl had a very serious expression on her face. "How many times do I have to do what, sweetie?" Gina asked.

"How many times do you have to be a bridesmaid before you get to be the bride?" Addie asked.

Gina laughed softly. She knew where this was coming from. "You've been talking to your grandmother, haven't you?"

Addie shook her head vigorously, sending her long, coal black hair bouncing from side to side.

"Uh-uh. Mama said you've been in a lot of weddings and that you were always a bridesmaid so I was just wondering when you get to stop being a bridesmaid and get to be a bride."

Judging by her expression, Gina could tell that it seemed like a logical progression of events to Addie.

Wiggling out of the bridesmaid dress, she draped it on the side of the bed as she threw on an old T-shirt and a pair of jeans. Dressed, Gina sat down on the bed and put her arm around her niece, pulling the little girl to her.

"That's not quite the way it works, sweetie," Gina said, managing not to laugh.

"You mean you're *always* going to be a bridesmaid?" Addie asked, her eyes opening so wide that she resembled one of her favorite stuffed animals. "Doesn't that make you sad?"

"No," Gina assured the little girl, rather touched that the girl was concerned about her. She hugged Addie closer. "It makes me happy."

The small, animated face scrunched up in confusion. "How come?"

She did her best to put it in terms that Addie could understand. "Being a bridesmaid is my job."

But it was obvious that this just confused Addie even more. "Being a bridesmaid is a job?"

"It is for me," Gina answered cheerfully. "The truth of it is, baby, for some people weddings can be very confusing and stressful."

Addie's smooth forehead was still wrinkled in consternation. "What's stressful?"

Gina thought for a moment. She didn't want to frighten the girl, but she did want to get the image across. "You know how when you play your video game and if you're not fast enough, suddenly the words *game over* can come on your screen and your tummy feels all knotted up and disappointed?"

"Uh-huh." Addie solemnly nodded her head.

"Well, that's what stressful is," Gina told her. "Organizing a wedding can be like that."

Addie looked at her uncertainly, doing her best to understand. "Weddings are like video games?"

A warm feeling came over Gina's heart and she grinned. "Sometimes. Your mom almost called off the wedding when she was marrying your dad. Everything suddenly felt as if it was just too much for her."

That had been the first time she had found herself coming to a bride's rescue. In that case it had been her older sister, Tiffany, who needed help. And that had been the beginning of an idea for a career.

"Really?" Addie asked in wonder.

"Really." Gina didn't emphasize how much of an emotional mess her normally level-headed older sister had been a few days before the wedding. "I saw what your mom was going through so I took over and helped her out. It was just a matter of untangling the order to the florist and maybe threatening the caterer," she added as more facts came back to her.

That really caught the little girl's attention. "Did you say you'd beat him up?" Addie asked in an impressed, hushed tone.

Gina laughed. "Worse. I threatened him with bad publicity."

Addie looked up at her in confusion. "What's bad pub-lis-ity?" she asked.

"Something everyone lives in fear of," Gina answered with a smile. "Anyway," she continued matter-of-factly, "I realized that I was pretty good at organizing things and that I could help brides like your mom really enjoy their day and not get caught up in the hassle." She decided that Addie didn't need to know anything beyond that. "And *that's* how your aunt Gina got the idea to became a professional bridesmaid."

"Can *I* become a professional bridesmaid?" Addie asked eagerly. It was obvious that her aunt's story had completely won her over.

"You have to get to be a little taller first," Gina told her, kissing the top of the girl's head. "But I don't see why you can't be one when you're grown up if you want to."

"Will you show me what to do once I get tall enough?" Addie asked seriously.

Gina inclined her head as if she was bowing to the little girl. "I'd be honored."

"Just what is it that you're going to show my daughter how to do once she gets tall enough?" Tiffany Loren asked as she came into the guest bedroom.

Addie swung around on the bed and looked up at her mother. "Aunt Gina's going to show me how to become a professional bridesmaid," she declared gleefully.

Tiffany looked more than a little dismayed. "Just what kind of ideas are you putting into my little girl's head?" she asked.

"I had nothing to do with it," Gina said, disavowing her culpability in the matter. "This was all Addie's idea."

"An idea she got from watching you come over here, parading around in all those bridesmaid dresses," Tiffany said pointedly.

"She could do worse," Gina answered defensively. "I get paid for making people happy and they get to enjoy their big day. Plus I get to eat cake on top of that. Not a bad gig if you ask me."

Tiffany looked at her daughter. This wasn't a conversation she wanted the little girl to hear. "Addie, why don't you go find your cousins? I want to talk to your aunt Gina for a minute."

Addie leaned in and told her aunt in a stage whisper, "Don't let her get you stressed, Aunt Gina."

Tiffany looked after her departing daughter, dumbfounded. "Where did that come from?" she asked her younger sister.

"I'd say she was just extrapolating on what I told her I did as a professional bridesmaid." Tiffany looked at her quizzically. "I told her that I made sure the bride didn't get stressed. I also might have told her that you were stressed on your wedding day—you were, you know," Gina reminded her sister before Tiffany could deny the fact or get annoyed with her.

Gina grinned as she thought about her niece. "I can't wait to hear how this is going to play itself out by the time Addie gets to tell her father about it." She flashed Tiffany a sympathetic smile.

"Terrific." Tiffany looked momentarily worried. "You know how Eddie jumps to conclusions."

"But you know how to get him to jump back and that's all that counts," Gina reminded her older sister. Her brother-in-law had a short fuse, but his outbursts never lasted too long.

Tiffany smiled to herself. "That I do. Can't wait until you get married so that I can pass along that wisdom and knowledge to you, little sister."

"About that, I wouldn't hold my breath if I were you," Gina advised. She saw the doubtful expression on Tiffany's face. "I'm perfectly happy with my life just the way it is."

Tiffany looked at her skeptically. "You'll forgive me if I don't believe you."

"That, dear Tiffany, is your prerogative. Now, if you'll excuse me, I have to prepare to hold a bride's hand and get her through what she'll remember as 'the happiest day of her life,' otherwise known as tomorrow."

"Do you have any more weddings lined up after that?" Tiffany asked her innocently.

"Not yet," Gina replied honestly. "But I will," she added with the confidence that she had managed to build up with this new career of hers.

Tiffany began to ease herself out of the bedroom. "By the way," she added, nodding at the dress on the bed, "you performed a miracle with that bridesmaid dress." She had seen the dress before its transformation. It had been absolutely ugly in her opinion.

"I know." There was no conceit in Gina's answer. There was just sheer pleasure in the knowledge that she was good at her chosen vocation.

Tiffany left the room, walking quickly. She waited until there was a room between her sister and her before she pulled her cell phone out of her pocket. Making sure that she was alone, she pressed auto-dial 8.

The line on the other end was picked up almost immediately.

"Mom?" Tiffany asked just to be sure she'd gotten the right person. When her mother answered in the affirmative, Tiffany declared, "All systems are 'go.' Gina's got nothing scheduled after she's done with this wedding."

"Perfect." The line went instantly dead.

Anna Bongino wasn't about to lose any time in calling her friend with the news.

"Gina has nothing immediately scheduled," Anna breathlessly told Maizie the moment the other woman answered her phone. "Whatever you're going to do, now would be the right time."

"I'll get back to you on this as soon as I can," Maizie promised.

Maizie had already gathered her best friends and comrades-in-arms together to tell them about Anna's daughter and her dissatisfaction that Gina was a perpetual professional bridesmaid. Intrigued, Celia Parnell and Theresa Manetti had gotten to work on the so-called "problem."

Maizie wasn't surprised that they already had a plan ready to go when she called Theresa with the news. A widow like Maizie and Celia, Theresa had built up a thriving catering service and she had found the perfect solution using that service.

"As luck would have it, the young bride whose reception I'm catering in three weeks is about to have a nervous breakdown," Theresa announced, sounding far happier than the news should have warranted.

"Why?" Maizie asked.

"It seems that her photographer somehow accidentally double-booked two ceremonies at the same time, one of them being my bride's. In addition, her cousin dropped out of the wedding at the last minute because her cousin's boyfriend of five years just broke up with her," Theresa explained.

"And we have just the young woman who can handle that for her and smooth out all the bumps," Maizie replied happily.

"Yes, we do," Theresa agreed.

"I admit that this does give us a reason to call Gina so she feels that her particular 'talents' are being utilized, but as far as I know, we still don't have any suitable candidates to play the potential groom to her potential bride-to-be—or do we?" Maizie asked when Theresa didn't immediately respond to her question.

"Hold on to your hat, Maizie. This is about to get even better," Theresa promised.

"All right, consider my hat held. *How* does this get even better?" Maizie asked.

She could almost hear Theresa smiling from ear to ear as she asked, "You know that young man Anna felt was so perfect for her daughter?"

"I remember. Shane Callaghan," Maizie recalled. "What about him?"

Theresa paused dramatically, then said, "Well, I found him."

"What do you mean you 'found' him?" Maizie asked suspiciously.

"Well, actually Celia did," Theresa amended. "He's a client of hers," she explained. "The fact is, 'Shane' has been using another name for his line of work."

This was all very mysterious to Maizie. "The point, Theresa. Get to the point," she told her friend impatiently.

That was when Theresa dropped her little bombshell. "It turns out that Shane Callaghan has a vocation that ties right into our little scenario. The man designs cakes—including wedding cakes—for a living—and he's very much in demand."

"Wouldn't Gina know this, seeing that she's in the business of placating jittery brides-to-be?" Maizie asked.

"That's where the pseudonym comes in. Shane is an 'artiste' known as Cassidy. His bakery is called Cakes Created by Cassidy."

She'd heard of it, Maizie realized. One of her clients had remarked that their son had ordered a cake from this "Cassidy." At the time she'd thought nothing of it.

"Really?" Maizie asked.

"Guess who I'm going to suggest to our bride to 'create' her wedding cake for her reception?" Theresa posed the rhetorical question almost gleefully.

This was playing it close, Maizie thought. "You said the wedding was in three weeks. Are you sure you can get him?"

"Absolutely," Theresa answered confidently. "It turns out that my son's law firm did some legal work for Cassidy a few months ago. It pays to have lunch with your offspring occasionally," she added, although she knew that none of them needed an excuse to get together with their children. Family had always been what this was all about for them, Theresa thought. "That's how I found out who Cassidy really is. It actually is a small world, Maizie," she declared happily. "Now all we need is to get Gina on the scene."

"Well, like I said," Maizie reminded her friend, "her mother just called me and said that Gina has nothing scheduled after this weekend's wedding."

"She does now," Theresa said happily. "I'd better get on the phone and talk to Sylvie—that's the bride-to-be—while she's still coherent. Her maid of honor said she was afraid that Sylvie was going to wind up calling the whole thing off."

"Something that she'll wind up regretting," Maizie predicted. "By all means, Theresa, call her. Tell her about Gina, that she can step in at the last minute and put out any fires that might arise. And then," she concluded, "you're going to have to call Gina."

"All right," Theresa agreed a bit uncertainly. "But why can't you call her?" she asked. After all Maizie was the one with a connection to the girl via Gina's mother.

"I'm a real estate agent, Theresa," Maizie reminded her friend. "There's no reason for me to know about a professional bridesmaid, whereas you, as a caterer with a multitude of wedding receptions to your credit, you could know about her through regular channels. Word of mouth, that kind of thing. If I called her up out of the blue with this offer, I'd have to admit to knowing her mother because how else would I know what she does for a living? She'd smell a rat and politely refuse. Or maybe not so politely," Maizie added.

"Goodness, this matchmaking hobby of ours has certainly gotten more complicated than it was back in the old days, hasn't it?" Theresa marveled.

"I know, but that's also part of the fun," Maizie reminded her friend. "Now stop talking to me and get on the phone to Gina and then to—what did you say was the bride-to-be's name?"

"Sylvie."

"Tell Sylvie you know just the person to step in and wind up saving her day," Maizie told her.

"Wait," Theresa cried, sensing that Maizie was about to hang up.

"What?"

"I need Gina's phone number," she told Maizie. "I can't tell Sylvie about this professional bridesmaid and then not have a phone number to pass on to her if she asks for it," Theresa pointed out. "Plus I'll need it myself if I'm going to set Gina up."

"Sorry," Maizie apologized as she retrieved the phone number from the file on her computer. "I guess I just got excited for a minute," she explained. "I *love* it when a plan comes together."

"So now we're the A-Team?" Theresa asked with an amused laugh. She was referring to an old television program she used to watch while waiting up for her workaholic lawyer husband to come home.

"The what?" Maizie asked, clearly not familiar with the program.

"Never mind about that right now. Just remind me that I have an old DVD to play for you when we all get a few minutes to ourselves."

"Will do," Maizie promised. "But right now, I'm

going to remind *you* that you have two phone calls to make. Possibly three," she amended.

"Three? How do you figure that?" Theresa asked her friend. "Do you want me to call you back once I get Gina and Sylvie?"

"Well, of course I want you to call me back to tell me how it all went. And then," Maizie continued, thinking out loud, "we have to come up with a way to have Gina and Shane get together before the big day. Maybe you can have Gina helping you with the arrangements, kind of like an assistant, and being a go-between for you and this 'in-demand baker.' And then, we can hope that there are sparks."

"A go-between?" Theresa questioned.

"We'll work on it," Maizie promised. "Now go, call while Gina's still free," she instructed her friend just before she hung up.

Chapter Two

Gina carefully hung up the light blue bridesmaid dress in her guest bedroom closet. The dress joined the vast and growing collection of other bridesmaid dresses, both long and short, that she had worn as part of the various bridal parties she'd been in. Because she had come in and in effect—at least in the bride's eyes—saved the wedding, she'd ultimately grown incredibly close to a number of the brides, not an easy feat in the space of two or three weeks.

Some of the brides had actually stayed in touch with her, at least for a little while. The others, though, had faded into the calendar of her life.

Even so, Gina had the satisfaction of knowing that because of her, more than a few women had experienced "the happiest day of their life" without having to endure the proverbial "glitch" that had a nasty habit of cropping up.

And despite what her mother thought of her rather unusual vocation, it did provide her with a nice living. In exchange for her services, she received more than ample compensation as well as another dress to hang in her closet, thanks to the bride, and, after the ceremony had ended and the photographs were taken, there was always a wonderful array of catered food to sample.

Not that she really ate all that much of it. Despite working almost nonstop in the weeks preceding the weddings, on the big day she never seemed to have that much of an appetite. It was almost as if she was channeling the bride's prewedding jitters even though she always appeared utterly calm and in complete control of the situation.

She supposed that was where her very brief flirtation with acting— or at least acting in her college plays— came in handy.

Gina sighed. With the latest wedding now behind her, she was, once again, unemployed.

She knew that she had word of mouth as well as a growing number of satisfied clients going for her, but even so she really needed to give some thought to building up her network, Gina decided. A network comprised of people who could call and alert her to brides in need of her very unique services.

Gina sank down on the bed, willing herself to wind down.

Each time she watched as the happy bride and groom finally drove off to begin their life together—starting with their honeymoon—amid the feeling of a job well done she also experienced just the faintest hint of feeling let down.

This time was no different. She knew her feelings

were silly and she tried not to pay any attention to them, but they were there nonetheless. That tiniest spark of wondering what it might have been like if she hadn't gotten cold feet and had instead agreed to run off with Shane that one wild, crazy night when he had suddenly turned to her and said, out of the blue, "Let's get married."

She supposed that her response—"Are you crazy?"— might have been a bit more diplomatic. But Shane had caught her off guard. They'd dated casually for two years but had only gotten serious in the last six months. When he'd asked her to marry him, the thought of doing something so permanent had scared her to death. She hadn't been ready for that sort of a commitment.

And he hadn't been ready for that kind of a total, harsh rejection. She'd regretted it almost instantly, but by then it had been too late. And she might have even said yes, she thought now. Or at least talked to him and suggested that they take things a little more slowly. But she hadn't been thinking clearly.

They had both just graduated from college that month and life was beginning to unfold for them. There were careers to launch and so many things to do before their lives even began to take shape.

In hindsight, all that uncertainty had frightened her, too. Loving Shane had been a comfortable thing, something for her to lean on. Loving Shane wasn't supposed to contribute to her feelings of being pressured.

Gina sighed. There was no point in going over all that now. By the time she'd worked up her nerve to apologize to Shane, to explain why she'd said what she had, it was too late. He'd taken off, vacating his apartment and leaving for parts unknown, just like that.

Nobody knew where he was.

Stop thinking about what you can't undo, she silently ordered herself. *It won't change anything.*

Dressed in her favorite outfit—cut-off jeans and a T-shirt—Gina went into her kitchen. She took out her favorite ice cream—rum raisin—and carried it into the living room. She settled down on the sectional sofa in front of her giant screen TV to binge-watch her favorite comedy series. She really needed a good laugh tonight.

Just as she turned on the set and pressed the necessary combination of buttons that got her to the first episode of the extensively long-running series—an episode she'd seen countless times before, whenever she was feeling down—her phone rang.

Gina looked at the cell accusingly. It was either someone trying to sell her some insurance—it was that time of year again she'd noticed—or it was her mother to pointedly ask her how "someone else's wedding" went and when did she think she would get around to planning one of her own.

Telling her mother that it would happen when she found someone to stand at the altar, waiting for her, never did any good because that only had her mother remembering how much she and the rest of the family had liked Shane. Shane had managed to endear himself to them in a very short amount of time. That was ten years ago and her mother still nostalgically referred to him as "the one who got away."

No, she definitely wasn't up to talking to her mother tonight.

Gina glanced at the caller ID. It wasn't her mother, or, from the looks of it, an insurance broker. The ID below the phone number proclaimed "Manetti's Catering."

The name seemed vaguely familiar. And then she remembered hearing the name on the radio along with the
slogan "Food like Mama used to make."

Curious, Gina set aside the half-pint of ice cream on
top of a section of the newspaper on her coffee table and
answered her phone.

"Hello?"

"Hello," a cheerful woman's voice on the other end
of the call responded. "Is this Gina Bongino?"

"Yes," Gina answered guardedly. "This is Gina."

She was prepared to terminate the call at a second's
notice if this turned out to be some clever telemarketer
who had matched her name to her cell number.

"Forgive me for bothering you so late on a Sunday,
but are you the same Gina Bongino who advertises herself as the Bridesmaid for Hire?" Theresa asked.

Before placing the call, Theresa had everything written down on a yellow pad and it was in front of her now.
She didn't want to take a chance on forgetting something or making a mistake. She, Maizie and Celia had
covered all the major points before she'd even placed
the call to Gina.

"I am," Gina answered, still wondering if this was
going to wind up being a crank call, or if this was actually on the level.

"Oh, thank goodness," Theresa declared. "You don't
know me, dear, but I'm Theresa Manetti. I run a catering service and I've done a good many wedding receptions. Especially lately."

"Yes?" Gina responded, waiting for the woman to get
to the point. She was hoping it involved what she did,
but you never knew. Maybe the woman was just looking for some advice. Or even a referral.

"I'll get right to the point," Theresa said as if reading her mind. "The reception I have coming up in three weeks just might wind up falling through. The poor girl who's the bride-to-be is about to have a nervous breakdown and I was wondering—" Stumbling, Theresa took a deep breath and glanced down at her notes. She started again. "Someone told me that you offer a very unique service. You come in and handle any emergency that might come up connected to the wedding so that the bride can enjoy a stress-free wedding day."

"That's right," Gina said, beginning to relax a little. This might be a job after all.

Schooling herself not to sound too eager, Theresa asked, "Just exactly what is it that you do?"

"Essentially, anything that needs to be done in order to make the wedding proceed as initially planned," Gina answered.

"Such as?" Theresa prompted.

Gina thought for a moment before framing her answer. "Such as anything from turning ugly bridesmaid dresses into flattering ones to lining up last-minute photographers to replace the one who dropped out. The same thing goes for hairdressers and makeup artists if the bride planned on having them. You name it, I've probably encountered it."

"Does that include being part of the wedding party? Because one of the bridesmaids suddenly just dropped out, leaving a lone groomsman," Theresa explained, checking off a line on her pad.

"I'm in the background," Gina explained. It was not her intention to take a chance on outshining any bride. "But yes, that's what the title implies. I actually am a bridesmaid for hire," she told the woman on the other end of the call.

She heard a large sigh of relief, something she was more than familiar with.

"Oh, you're a godsend," Theresa declared, and she was only half acting.

"I will need to talk to the bride herself to make sure she's on board," Gina told the caller before things progressed any further. "To be honest, it's usually the bride or a member of her family who hires me. I've never had a caterer ask me to help out the bride before," she said.

"Oh, I quite understand and I realize this is unusual, but then, so's a bridesmaid for hire," Theresa pointed out.

"Can't argue with you there," Gina agreed with a soft laugh.

"I did talk to Sylvie about you as soon as I became aware that there was someone like you who did this kind of thing," Theresa explained. "And she told me to go ahead and see if she could hire you. As I said, the wedding's in three weeks and it seems like everything that could go wrong at this point has."

She'd dealt with situations like that before, Gina thought. "As long as the bride and groom are there, the rest can be managed," she assured the motherly sounding woman on the other end.

"Well, with your help, I'm sure that they'll be there all right," Theresa told her, smiling to herself. This was actually going to work, she thought. Wait until she called Maizie and Celia. "And they're such a cute couple. They're really made for each other."

The woman sounded more like a mother than a caterer, Gina thought. "Sounds good," she told Theresa.

"Now, if you can give me the particulars, I'll place the call to—Sylvie is it?"

"It's Sylvia, actually. Sylvia Stevens, but everyone just calls her Sylvie. She looks like a Sylvie," Theresa told her. There was a fond note in her voice that Gina immediately picked up on.

"Give me her cell number and her address and I'll give her a call first thing in the morning to make the arrangements," Gina said.

Theresa gave her the information, enunciating everything slowly so that Gina didn't miss a thing. "I want you to know that you're the answer to a prayer," she added with just the right amount of feeling. She didn't really have to pretend all that much. After all, Sylvie *was* going to pieces.

"It'll be my pleasure to do whatever needs to be done to make sure Sylvie has as perfect a wedding day as humanly possible," Gina assured the woman.

"Speaking of which, there is just one more thing," Theresa said. She'd saved the most important part for last because she wanted to make sure that Gina was fully engaged in this endeavor before she told the young woman about this part.

Gina had no idea why, but she could feel herself suddenly bracing. What was the woman going to ask for? "Yes?"

"I'm going to be short staffed for the rest of the month—" Theresa began, easing her way into this final chapter.

Gina wanted to quickly stop the woman before this went any further. "I'm afraid that catering the reception is a little out of my league, Mrs. Manetti. Especially if

I'm going to be in the wedding party and seeing to other details," she told Theresa.

"Oh no, dear, it's nothing like that," Theresa was quick to assure her. "The fact of the matter is, the bride requested to have her cake done by this cake designer she heard about. His work is in high demand. Perhaps you've heard of him as well?" Theresa asked, hoping against hope that Gina's answer would be negative. "Cakes Created by Cassidy."

Theresa held her breath, waiting for Gina's response. She caught herself crossing her fingers as the seconds ticked by.

"No," Gina finally admitted. "I can't say that I have," she added, still waiting to find out just what it was that Theresa was going to ask her to do.

Theresa slowly released the breath she'd been holding, being careful not to alert the young woman on the other end that there was anything out of the ordinary going on.

"Well, because I have all these other catering affairs between now and Sylvie's wedding, I was wondering if you could handle ordering the cake from this Cassidy person. Sylvie will give you all her requirements when you talk to her."

The request was doable, but it struck her as being a little strange. "Wouldn't she and the groom want to sample the cake before they put in their final order?" Gina asked.

In her experience, the bride and groom usually sampled a great many cakes before they settled on their final choice.

"Oh no," Theresa quickly shot down the idea. "Sylvie worked furiously to diet down so that she could fit into this dress. Now that she's the right size, she's desperately trying *not* to gain any weight between now and the wedding. That also includes not doing *any* cake sampling."

Theresa paused for a second to catch her breath before continuing. "That would be what she wanted you for, along with an entire myriad of other bride-related things that ordinarily don't add up to that much but right now, as I told you, Sylvie is tottering on the brink of a nervous breakdown. To be honest, no one knows what might just push her over the edge. Would you mind terribly meeting with this cake designer and taking care of this for her?"

"Eating a slice of cake made by an in-demand cake decorator? No, not a bit," Gina answered with a laugh. She glanced over at her melting rum raisin. "Is there anything else, Mrs. Manetti?"

"No, nothing I can think of at the moment," Theresa answered breezily.

"Then thank you for the call and the opportunity. I'll get right on this tomorrow morning," she said again. "And I'll call you once I speak with Sylvie."

"Wonderful. And I look forward to meeting you in person, dear," Theresa told her. "And again, I'm sorry for having to call so late but I just got off the phone with Sylvie and I knew that something needed to be done quickly."

She did have one question. "Who told you about me again?" Gina asked. The woman hadn't been quite clear as to who had given the caterer her name when she'd first called.

Theresa quickly checked her notes, finding the name that she was told to use.

"Virginia Gallagher told me about you, although her

name is Price now. The Gallagher-Price wedding," she threw in to substantiate her story.

Gina thought for a moment. "I was in that wedding party over a year ago," she remembered.

"And Virginia—she's a friend of my daughter's—is still singing your praises," Theresa said, hoping that would seal the deal.

She knew that she and her two coconspirators in matchmaking needed to make sure that Gina didn't suspect anything was amiss as she engaged the professional bridesmaid's services to help smooth out another wedding in possible turmoil. That meant not focusing too much on the additional assignment of selecting the cake. The whole idea here was to get her down to the Cakes Created by Cassidy shop so she could cross paths with Shane after all these years.

From everything that she and her friends had managed to uncover, Gina and Shane had once been the absolute epitome of a perfect match and for all intents and purposes, it seemed that they still were. They just needed to be made to realize that again.

"Oh, and I intend to pay you extra for this cake service you'll be performing since technically, it isn't something you would ordinarily do," Theresa interjected, hoping that would do the trick.

But Theresa hadn't counted on Gina's integrity. "How's that again? You want to pay me extra for procuring the wedding cake."

Theresa hesitated for a moment. "Well, the caterer usually provides the cake unless the bride has other ideas."

"Wouldn't that still come out of the bride's pocket—

so to speak? That makes it part of the package deal between the bride and me," Gina concluded.

"Perhaps, but I don't want Sylvie stressing out any more than she already is," Theresa said, hoping that would satisfy Gina and put an end to any further questions, at least for the time being. "We'll talk more tomorrow, dear," Theresa promised just before she quickly terminated the call.

Strange, Gina thought. But then, so was what she did for a living. Especially in her mother's eyes. The bottom line was that she was employed again.

This was good. This was very, very good.

She could feel herself growing enthusiastic, the way she always did at the beginning of a new assignment.

She looked over toward the coffee table. Her ice cream had turned into soup.

Getting up, Gina picked up the rum raisin container and took it back to the freezer so that she could turn the soup back into ice cream again.

She was whistling as she went.

Chapter Three

Gina felt that her phone call to Sylvie the next morning went well.

Just as she'd been warned, she found that the anxious young woman she spoke to was indeed two steps away from becoming a bridezilla.

Speaking in a slow, calm voice, Gina made arrangements to meet with the woman early the following morning. She promised Sylvie that everything would turn out just the way she wanted, then proceeded to give her a few examples of other weddings she had successfully handled.

Listening, Sylvie seemed to noticeably calm down. She sounded almost eager to look up Gina's website to read what other brides had posted about their own weddings and how potential disasters-in-the-making had been successfully averted, thanks to a few well-executed efforts.

By the time she hung up, Gina was fairly certain that Sylvie had calmed down sufficiently to be downgraded from the level of "bridezilla" to an almost normal, anxious bride-to-be.

While talking to Sylvie, she'd gotten very specific directions about the kind of multitiered wedding cake the bride and groom had their hearts set on—although she strongly suspected that the groom's "heart" wasn't nearly as involved in this choice as the bride's was. She'd even had to promise Sylvie that she'd stop by the bakery to engage this so-called sought-after cake "artiste" known as Cassidy right after she ended their call.

All in all, Gina thought, pressing the end call button on her cell, this was shaping up to be a really productive day.

But before she did anything else, she decided as she grabbed her purse and her squadron of keys, she needed to stop at Manetti's Catering. It was only right for her to thank the woman who had sent this new bit of business her way.

Because of its ever-expanding clientele, the catering company had recently moved out of its former rather small, confining quarters to a genuine homey-looking shop where the shop's homemade pastries and sandwiches-to-go could be properly showcased and also seen through the large bay windows.

Located in the heart of an upscale shopping center, the sight of the food enticed shoppers to come in, sample, and, ideally, be inspired to book a future party ranging from small and intimate to a blow-out bash.

Walking into the shop, Gina was impressed by what she saw and exceedingly pleased that she had managed to catch the attention of someone like Theresa Manetti. She was certain that if she came through for Sylvie, Mrs.

Manetti could be counted on to throw more business her way down the line.

It never hurt to network, Gina thought.

"May I help you?" a soft, almost melodic voice asked, coming from behind the counter.

"Hi, I'm Gina Bongino—the professional brides-maid," she answered, tagging on her signature label, hoping that would mean something to the older woman.

Coming around the counter, the thin woman with salt-and-pepper hair took her hand in hers. "Gina, what a pleasure to meet you. I'm Theresa Manetti."

Gina's first thoughts were that the woman looked just the way she had sounded on the phone last night. Warm and gracious. And genuine.

Gina found herself eager to please the caterer who she had taken an immediate liking to.

Theresa took out a folded piece of paper from her apron pocket. "I've written everything down for you," she told Gina, tucking the paper into her hand. "That's the baker's name, phone number, the address of the shop and, of course, the kind of wedding cake Sylvie wants at her wedding."

Gina glanced at the paper, nodding. "She already de-scribed it to me when I talked to her this morning," she told Theresa.

"Well, it never hurts to have it written down in front of you," Theresa said with a smile. "I'd take care of this my-self," she told Gina again, "but as I've already mentioned to you last night, we are extremely busy these days."

As if to bear her out, there was continuous noise com-ing from the back of the shop. Gina guessed that was where the kitchen was located and the woman's employ-ees were undoubtedly all busy working.

Gina caught herself being very grateful that fate had somehow brought them together. She was *sure* that Theresa Manetti could throw a little business her way down the line.

"Don't worry about a thing, Mrs. Manetti," Gina replied. "I'll take care of ordering the cake and everything else that I gathered Sylvie needed done." She tucked away the paper Theresa had handed her into her purse. "I just wanted to come by and say thank you," she explained.

"I'm the one who should be thanking you," Theresa told her. "My fees are nonrefundable, so it's not a matter of my losing money. But I have to admit I get personally involved with all my clients and I really do want them, if at all possible, to come away happy and satisfied."

Gina could only smile at the woman. It wasn't often she heard someone espousing something as selfless as that. Again she found herself thinking that she liked Theresa Manetti right from the start.

"I have a feeling that this is the beginning of a wonderful friendship," she told Theresa, preparing to leave.

"I certainly hope so, dear," Theresa replied, the corners of her eyes crinkling as she smiled. "I certainly hope so," she repeated as the door closed on the departing enterprising bridesmaid for hire.

Following Theresa's directions, Gina made her way to another, smaller shopping center. This one was located on the far side of Bedford. She briefly entertained the idea of calling ahead but decided against it. She wanted to be there on the premises in case she had to convince this "Cassidy" to accept the order and have it ready by the day of the wedding.

She knew from experience that people who fancied themselves to be "artistes" were, for the most part, temperamental and constantly needed to have their egos stroked. She had learned that stroking was best done in person.

So Gina went over to the Fairview Plaza where the shop was located, parked in the first empty parking space she saw, and set out to find the bakery and this Cassidy who created works of art that could be eaten with a fork.

The store was so small and unassuming, she missed it on her first pass through the center. She was searching for something eye-catching and ostentatious.

The shop, when she found it on her second time around, was neither. It was a small white shop with blue lettering and it was nestled in between a children's toy store and a trendy store selling overpriced organic fruits and vegetables.

Gina looked over the outside as she stood in front of the entrance. "Well, either ego's not his problem or the rent's really cheap here," she speculated.

There were no hours posted on the door, so she had no idea if it was open or not. Maybe she *should* have called ahead, she thought.

Trying the doorknob, Gina found that the door was open. Coming in, her entrance was heralded by the light tinkling of an actual bell that was hanging right over the front door rather than a buzzer or a symphony of virtual chimes.

It was almost charming, she thought. Probably to catch the customer off guard so that they wouldn't think fast enough to protest being hit with an oversize price tag for a cake that could have just as easily been made out of a couple of everyday, standard box mixes.

At first glance, there was no one in the front of the store. She did, however, see a partially closed door that led to what she presumed was the back where "all the magic happened."

"Hello?" Gina called out, raising her voice slightly. "Is anyone here?"

Listening, she heard movement coming from the back. Maybe it was the person who took the cake orders, she thought. Odd that they didn't come out when the bell sounded.

When no one came out to the showroom, Gina tried again.

"I'd like to order a wedding cake for a wedding taking place three weeks from now."

Actually, it was three weeks from this past Saturday, she thought, but that was a tidbit she was going to save until she had someone in front of her she could make eye contact with.

The movement she'd initially heard had definitely stopped. And still no one opened the back door any farther. Weren't they coming out?

This was all very strange, she thought. Maybe this "artiste" wasn't here and she had walked in on a misguided burglar who was caught in the act of trying to rob the place.

She tried one last time. Raising her voice again, Gina called out, "If this is a bad time, I'll come back. You don't have your store hours posted, but—"

She saw the door leading to the back room opening all the way.

Finally, she thought.

And then, when she saw the person walking to the front of the shop—walking toward *her*—her jaw slackened, causing her mouth to drop open. Any other sound that might have come out at that point didn't.

After a beat, Gina realized that she had forgotten to breathe.

Shane.

But it couldn't be.

Could it?

And yet… It was definitely Shane, cutting the distance between them in what now felt like slow motion.

Was she dreaming?

She would have blinked to clear her eyes if it didn't strike her as being almost cartoon-like.

A hot wave washed over her.

Breathe, damn it. Breathe! she silently ordered herself.

When he heard her voice, Shane was almost convinced that he was imagining things. He had come out to see and prove himself wrong.

Even so, he knew he would have recognized *her* voice anywhere.

And he was right.

It *was* her.

Ten years went up in smoke and just for an instant, he was that lovesick kid again.

And then reality, with all its harsh reminders, returned with a vengeance.

"Hello, Gina."

Because for one wild split second, the shop she was standing in had insisted on going for a quick spin around her, Gina grabbed the edge of the counter to keep herself steady. She refused to do something so incredibly hokey as to pass out even though she felt as if she could barely get her legs to support her.

"Shane?" she whispered.

His name slipped out before she could stop herself. It *looked* like Shane, except that it was a handsomer, upgraded version of the man who lived ten years, un-changed, in her past. His face appeared more gaunt now, and more rugged. Some of the boyishness had worn away, replaced, she noted, by an almost arousing manliness.

His hair was still blond, though, and his eyes, his eyes were still that piercing shade of blue that always seemed to go right through her. Time hadn't changed that, she thought.

The corners of his mouth curved ever so slightly at the confusion that was on her face.

"Don't tell me you've forgotten what I look like," he said in response to the questioning way she had said his name.

Oh God, no, Gina thought. Even if she had gotten am-nesia, there was no way she could *ever* forget Shane's face. Like it or not, it was and always would be permanently embossed on her brain.

Because she realized that she was staring at him as if he were an apparition, Gina cleared her throat and stumbled her way through an explanation.

"I'm sorry—" she began only to have him interrupt her.

"Nice to finally hear you say that," Shane said.

Gina wasn't able to read his expression, but she in-stantly pulled her shoulders back, prepared to engage in an unpleasant exchange. Not that, at least from his point of view, she could actually fault him. But in her own defense, she had tried to find him and apologize. But she wasn't able to and that was *his* fault. He was the one who had taken off and disappeared, not her.

"—but I seem to be in the wrong place," Gina con-tinued tersely. "I'm looking for a cake designer named Cassidy—"

Shane inclined his head. For now, he stayed behind

the counter. He didn't trust himself to come any closer to Gina than he was at this moment. Despite the fact that he felt she had humiliated him, despite being angry at her, the woman had still managed to fill his head, not to mention his dreams, every waking minute for more than an entire year.

It had taken that much time for his longing to subside, and then another year for him to pull himself together. That was when he admitted to himself that he didn't want to be a lawyer. That had once been his parents' dream, not his, even though he'd tried to honor it. So one day he just walked away from it, had gone to work with his older brother halfway around the world and ultimately found something he felt he had a passion for. Something unique and unlike anything he had ever done before.

Myriad emotions pulsed through Shane right now as he looked at Gina, although he was able to keep any of that from registering on his face.

Instead, he told Gina in a very calm voice, "I'm Cassidy."

Gina stared at him, her eyebrows coming together almost in an upside down V. What was he trying to put over on her?

"No, you're not," she contradicted, almost annoyed that he was trying to fool her. "You're Shane."

Just saying his name again after all this time sent ripples of warmth and longing undulating through her. Her brain was having trouble computing seeing him after all this time. At the very least, the man should have had the decency to look a little paunchy and worn around the edges, not like some rugged movie star stepping off the big screen.

And why was he smiling at her like that? Was he going to say something sarcastic?

"You don't remember," Shane guessed.

"Remember what?" she asked, feeling more and more confused, befuddled and exasperated.

This morning, she had been happily saving yet another anxious bride's wedding, and now, less than a couple of hours later, she felt as if she was suddenly caught up in the center of a whirlpool, being tossed around and unable to figure out which way was up.

"That my middle name is Cassidy," he went on to tell her. "Shane Cassidy Callaghan," he said, giving her his full name as he watched her face.

Seeing Gina again without any warning just served to remind him how much he had missed looking at that face. How much he had missed the scent of her hair and the feel of her soft body pressed against his.

Get a grip, Callaghan. She did a number on you once, don't leave yourself open for another assault. She's even forgotten your middle name.

But that didn't surprise him. She'd undoubtedly forgotten a great many things about him, Shane thought. And about the two of them.

Things that he *couldn't* forget no matter how much he tried.

"Then Cakes Created by Cassidy is your company?" she asked him, not bothering to hide her disbelief.

Gina was having a great deal of trouble processing any of it. Not just seeing him again, but the rest of it, as well.

A cake designer? Really? Shane?

The Shane she'd known back in college had occasionally slipped her notes with drawings of the two of them at the bottom. She recalled that he liked to draw. But back then the only thing he was capable of doing in the kitchen was opening the refrigerator door.

How had he gone from kitchen illiterate to a master baker?

"It's catchy, don't you think?" Shane asked. There was a touch of pride in his voice that she found hard to miss now.

"More like incredible," she admitted.

"That's a word I usually hear *after* someone has sampled one of my cakes." Before she could say anything, Shane changed the conversation's direction. "When you walked in, you said something about coming here to order a wedding cake."

She was almost grateful to him. It was as if he had snapped his fingers, getting her out of her mental haze and forcing her to focus on the reason she had come here in the first place. The sooner she stated it, the sooner she could get away.

"Right." She took out the paper that Theresa had given her. The cake's specifications were written in the woman's rather striking handwriting. She focused on it now. "I need to have this cake made and delivered to the Blue Room at the Bedford Hilton Hotel by two o'clock." Pointing to the line on the paper, she said, "I need it by that date. That's in three weeks."

He didn't bother looking at the paper. "I know when it is—"

"Good then." She left the paper on the counter for him. "You can send the bill to—"

"—and it's not possible," Shane said, completing his sentence.

Caught off guard, she stared at him, wondering if she'd heard him correctly. "Excuse me?"

"I said that it's not possible," Shane repeated in the same quiet, calm voice.

"What do you mean it's not possible?" Gina demanded. "I'm giving you three weeks' notice."

"I know," Shane responded, unfazed. "And I'm booked solid."

Was he bragging? Okay, she'd let him have his moment. All things considered, he deserved it. She had never wished him ill. She looked around, noticing for the first time that there were framed photographs on the walls. None of him, she noted, but of some of the cakes he had created.

The one that caught her eye was amazingly constructed in the shape of the Eiffel Tower. How did someone even begin to do that? she wondered, stunned.

She looked at Shane, utterly impressed. "You're doing well, I see."

Shane nodded and replied without a trace of bravado, "Very well, thanks."

"And I'm happy for you," she told him—and she meant it, aside from attempting to get on his good side for the sake of her client. "Surely you can squeeze in one more cake."

She couldn't read the expression on his face. But there was no misunderstanding his words. "No," he replied flatly. "Sorry."

Chapter Four

He couldn't be serious, Gina thought.

"But it's just one cake," she argued, unable to believe that Shane, or whatever he chose to call himself these days, couldn't find a way to make this important cake a reality. "It's not even anything especially elaborate, like that tower or bridge," she said, gesturing at the photographs of cakes he had made. "Just a lot of tiers and your signature swirl around the edges." Theresa had told her that Sylvie insisted on the swirls.

But Shane remained steadfast and shook his head again, turning her request down. "Sorry."

He wasn't sorry at all, Gina thought. This had to be his way of getting back at her after all this time. Well, she had no intentions of having her client wind up paying for something that she had done a decade ago.

"Why won't you do it?" she asked. She knew that if

she came back and told Sylvie that she wasn't able to get her cake for the wedding—failing so early in their association—the bride was just going to fall to pieces and most likely fire her. This was becoming a challenge for her. "What if I pay you twice the amount that you normally charge?" Gina proposed. "Will you find a way to do it then?"

But Shane remained unmoved. "Sorry, Gina. You're going to have to just find someone else to bake your cake for your big day."

Was that it? Did he think that she was asking him to make *her* wedding cake? Gina was quick to set him straight. "The cake isn't for me."

"Right," Shane replied sarcastically. "It's for everyone at the reception." He'd heard that approach before.

"Well, technically, yes," Gina agreed. She was right, she thought. Shane did think she was asking for him to bake her wedding cake. She could see how he felt that she was rubbing salt into his wounds, even after all this time. "But if you don't make this cake, in less than three weeks, there is going to be one unhappy bride who will be having a nervous breakdown because she is going to feel that her big day is just crumbling all to pieces right in front of her."

Gina saw something in Shane's eyes that she couldn't quite make out, and then he shrugged, unmoved. "I'm sorry but there's nothing I can do for you, Gina. I'm booked solid. You'll just have to eat someone else's cake at your wedding."

A fresh wave of guilt washed over her. Had she hurt him that much? Over the years, when she couldn't locate him, she'd talked herself into believing that he really hadn't cared.

But he had, she realized.

"It's not my wedding, Shane," she told him quietly.

About to go back into the kitchen area and send out one of his assistants to usher her out, Shane stopped and turned around again.

"Wait, what?" he asked. Was she lying, trying to get him to agree to create one of his signature cakes for her, or was she being truthful?

"I said it's not my wedding," Gina repeated, slowly enunciating every word.

This didn't make any sense to him. Shane was accustomed to having the bride—usually accompanied by the groom—be the one who placed the order for the cake. And this was only after an unusual amount of deliberation and questions, not to mention cake sampling, took place. If Gina wasn't the bride, then what was she doing placing the order for the wedding cake?

"All right," he said gamely. "Whose wedding is it?" he asked.

"The bride's name is Sylvie Stevens," she answered, adding, "Right now, quite honestly, the groom's name escapes me."

Most of the miscellaneous thoughts that usually resided in her head had all inexplicably vanished, leaving her to fend for herself. The reason for that was because she had run into Shane in the least likely place she would have ever thought of seeing him. In a shop that he apparently owned and operated as a creative baker. All of this had left her practically incoherent and totally unprepared to deal with any of this.

"This Sylvie Stevens," Shane said, picking up on the bride's name, "is she a relative of yours?"

There was no doubt about it. Shane felt as if he was

groping around in the dark, trying to find the door so he could get out.

He was fairly certain that he had met all of Gina's relatives during the time that they had been together. As he recalled, it wasn't that big a family. He knew he would have remembered someone named Sylvie.

"No—" Gina began.

He cut her off. "A friend, then?" he asked in disbelief. This was really an unusual circumstance if she was making the decision for a friend. Despite his initial decision to just close the door on Gina the way she had so callously closed it on him, Shane found his curiosity aroused. "Are you here making arrangements for a cake for a friend?"

Saying yes would have been the easy way out, but Gina knew her best bet was to be totally honest with him. "I can't call this bride-to-be my friend, although some of my clients do wind up that way by the time the wedding takes place."

He stared at her. He hadn't a clue what she was talking about.

"You've lost me," Shane told her impatiently.

His choice of words vividly brought back the past to her.

I did, didn't I? Gina thought, a huge pang of regret twisting her stomach. She really wished that there was such a thing as a do-over button she could press.

She took a breath. "Maybe I should explain," she began.

"Maybe you should," Shane agreed crisply.

He silently warned himself not to get caught up in any of this. That meant that he couldn't allow the sound of her voice to get to him or allow the way he had once felt about her to influence him in any way.

But despite everything, Shane had to admit that his curiosity had been aroused in a big way.

Gina took another deep breath before telling him, "I'm a professional bridesmaid."

His reaction was the same sort she had become used to getting. "What the hell is that?" Shane demanded.

"Just what it sounds like," she told him. "Simply put, I hire out my services to prospective brides. I promise them that I will take care of any and all possible emergencies that might arise before and during the ceremony. Emergencies that could derail what the bride had envisioned as her perfect day."

Gina's explanation had almost rendered him speechless.

Almost.

"You're kidding," Shane said, recovering. "You, the woman who couldn't commit herself to the man who foolishly bared his soul to her, *you're* in charge of making other people's weddings a success?" he asked incredulously.

There it was again, Gina thought, that wave of guilt that threatened to all but drown her. "Shane, I can't tell you how much—"

Shane upbraided himself for dropping his guard and allowing this to get personal. Aware of his error, Shane waved away what he could tell was going to be another apology. He didn't want to hear it. The damage had long since been done and they had both moved on.

As possibly a direct result of her rejection, he had forged a better version of himself and had gone on to create a career out of the ashes that was far more satisfying to him than the path he had been set to follow when she'd suddenly stomped on his heart.

"Never mind all that now," Shane told her rather formally. "This cake you're trying to order, it *isn't* for you?" he asked, wanting to be totally sure before continuing.

"No, it's not. And Sylvie really does seem to have her heart set on you being the one making this cake for her." And then she added what she hoped would be the argument that would tip the scales in Sylvie's favor. "If you won't make the cake, it's almost as if the rest of her wedding is doomed."

Shane laughed shortly at the absurdity of what she'd just said. "That's a little dramatic and over-the-top, don't you think?" he asked.

For the first time, Gina laughed in response. He found the sound disturbing in a way he definitely didn't want to be disturbed.

"You'd be surprised what some of these brides are like and what they say when they feel stressed," Gina told him, extrapolating on this momentary temporary truce that they had struck. "The term *bridezilla* is not just some whimsical, weird name that someone dreamed up. It's actually rather an accurate description of the transformation that some of these perfectly sane women undergo when dealing with the one hundred–plus miscellaneous details that comprise pulling off the perfect wedding," she told him.

"Just as an example," Gina went on to say, "suddenly the size and color of the table napkins take on a whole new meaning. Weddings put enormous pressure on the bride and on the people around the bride who are trying to emotionally support her."

He supposed, although he hadn't given it much

thought, he could see that happening. "If that's the case, why not just go to a wedding planner?" he asked.

"Some do," Gina agreed. "But I'm actually less expensive and in many cases, a lot friendlier. I'm more like a paid best friend, there to listen and to hold the bride's hand for the duration ranging from just before the wedding to the three or four weeks leading up to the big day, depending on when I'm called in."

He thought about her description, even though he had never heard of what she did being a profession before. "So this is really on the level?" Shane asked her again as he began to come around.

Gina didn't hesitate for a second. "Absolutely," she assured him.

"Exactly how many of you 'professional bridesmaids' are there out there?" he asked.

She had to admit that she didn't know of anyone who did what she did. She had come up with this on her own while brainstorming one afternoon, going over all the different skills she had developed. Being a bridesmaid all those different times had stood out head and shoulders above the rest.

"As far as I know, there's just me," Gina replied. She saw the skeptical look on Shane's face. "Oh, since there's really nothing new under the sun, I'm sure there might be some other professional bridesmaids out there. But for now, I'm the only one I know of doing this sort of thing. At least in this state." That much she had researched recently. "Anything else you'd like to know?" she asked Shane.

More things than you could possibly begin to answer in the space of time we have today, Shane thought as he tried not to stare at her.

Old memories kept trying to break through and he blocked them.

"No," he replied. "That answers my questions. For now."

An ominous feeling swept over Gina, but she fiercely pushed it away. She couldn't afford to get caught up in anything right now. She needed to focus on the immediate business at hand.

And Shane still hadn't given her the answer she needed. "So, will you do it?" she asked. "Will 'Cassidy' create one of his much sought-after cakes for Sylvie, thereby making her an extremely happy, albeit still anxious bride?" Gina asked, never taking her eyes off Shane's face.

He didn't answer right away. As a matter of fact, he was silent for so long, Gina was beginning to think that maybe she *hadn't* won him over.

If she were to guess what was happening, she would have said that Shane was relishing having to turn her down.

But just as she had resigned herself to the inevitable, he flashed a small smile at her and said, "I'll do it. On one condition."

Gina braced herself. This was going to be something that had to do with her. Shane was going to exact some sort of an act of contrition from her for having turned him down a decade ago. Okay, as long as it wasn't anything incredibly humiliating, she was willing to go through with whatever he came up with, jumping through any hoops he cited.

She owed it to him—and to her client.

"Name it," she said, holding her breath.

"I need to meet with the bride and groom," Shane told

her in no uncertain terms. "Or at least with the bride. Both would be preferable, but meeting with the one is nonnegotiable."

Gina expected a wave of relief to engulf her when she heard Shane's terms. But the relief she would have expected to experience at being taken off the hook like this didn't quite materialize and she had no idea why. Somehow, given all this, she felt as if she'd just been shoved into limbo with the proverbial door being slammed shut on her.

Maybe all this guilt she'd been carrying around in her mind had no real reason to exist after all. It was a possibility, she told herself.

"You want to meet with the bride," she repeated just to be certain she understood what Shane was asking for and there were no unspoken, hidden terms that she wasn't getting.

"Yes, I want to meet with the bride." With a sigh, he explained his reasons behind the term. "I don't just 'bake' a wedding cake. I create it. And creating a wedding cake for a couple is a very personal thing. To do it effectively, to give the couple their proper due, I need to meet with at least the bride to make sure I get it right and capture the essence of the two people getting married."

She wanted to point out that the ingredients would wind up being the same no matter how the couple struck him or what he thought of them. But to avoid any arguments, she kept that to herself. She'd just scored a huge win here in getting him to agree to make the wedding cake at all. She knew she couldn't risk doing something to turn him off and make him change his mind about making this cake for Sylvie.

"Sure," Gina agreed readily. "Just tell me when it's

convenient for you and I'll arrange for Sylvie to come to your shop to meet with you." She paused for a second and then, knowing she was going out on a limb here, she added, "And with any luck, her future husband, too."

There was still part of Shane that thought this was all a creative hoax on her part. That she had made it all up. That meant that there was no "Sylvie," no wedding and definitely not that ridiculous position she had just told him about: a professional bridesmaid.

But he had never been a conceited man and to actually believe Gina had gone to all this trouble just to worm back into his life would be just that, conceited.

No, as absurd as this sounded to him, Shane thought, this had to be on the level. And, if he was being honest, he supposed that her job was no more unusual than what he did—creating extremely unique cakes for people to celebrate all different occasions.

"Wait right here," he told her. "Let me check my calendar."

The next moment, he turned and walked into the back room he had initially been in when she had entered his shop.

Gina watched the door close. She couldn't help wondering if he was stepping out of her life again, just as he had the last time he had walked out and closed the door on her.

She knew that sounded paranoid, but given their history, she couldn't help the thoughts that were rearing their heads in her mind.

When the door opened again a couple of minutes later, Gina almost blew out an audible sigh of relief.

He saw the look on her face before she managed to

sublimate it. "You didn't think I was coming back, did you?" he asked.

"No," she denied. "I was just wondering what was taking you so long." She could feel his eyes looking at her knowingly. "Most people have their calendars on their smartphones, not somewhere in the back room," she explained, saying the first thing that came to her head.

His shrug was offhanded and casual. "I guess I'm not like most people," he told her.

She thought of the way he had been all those years ago and the unusual path his life had taken now. "No," she agreed. "That you definitely are not."

Damn it, why was her heart pounding like this? She needed to get a grip on herself before she said or did something to make a complete fool of herself.

Clearing her throat, Gina forced herself to think strictly about the wedding she was now responsible for and only that.

"So, did you find a date that's good for you?" she asked him cheerfully. "To meet with Sylvie," she added when he didn't respond.

"Well, as I said, my schedule is crowded." As if to prove it, he glanced at his watch and unconsciously took a step toward the back door again. "I've got a cake I need to get started creating even now."

"Then I won't keep you," Gina promised. "Just give me a date and I'll get out of your hair just like that." She snapped her fingers.

I did give you a date. And you didn't want it.

The thought suddenly popped up in his mind, totally unbidden.

This was a mistake, Shane told himself. He should have just referred her to another baker right from the beginning. But he had painted himself into a corner and now he was going to have to live with the consequences.

With any luck, he consoled himself, once this cake was made and delivered, he would never have to see Gina again.

That was what he wanted, right? What they *both* wanted. Right?

Shane realized she was looking at him, waiting for him to say something. Oh right, she was waiting for him to come up with a date.

"Wednesday at ten work for you?" he asked.

She had no idea what Sylvie's schedule was like because she hadn't even met with the woman yet. It didn't matter. Whatever Sylvie had to do could be moved around and dealt with. The bride had implied that this cake was all-important to her and meeting Shane was what it was going to take to make it a reality.

"I'll make it work," Gina told him.

And then she finally fled the shop the way she'd been wanting to from the moment she had seen that Shane and Cassidy were one and the same.

Chapter Five

It wasn't until Gina sat down behind the wheel of her car and closed the driver's side door that it finally hit her. When it did, she felt as if she was experiencing the effects of a ten-megaton bomb going off, catching her dead center.

Shane Callaghan.

Wow. After all these years of wondering what had happened to him, after having him haunt her dreams for at least a year of that time, their paths had finally crossed.

Well, at least he hadn't wasted away in some lonely, one-room hunting cabin, pining for her. That had been one of the concerns that had bothered her over the years when she couldn't locate him.

She had really tried to find out what happened to Shane after she had turned him down and he had totally disappeared. But at the time finding someone to ask about him had been impossible. The friends he'd sometimes spent time with had all moved away after graduation to start their new lives. Shane's parents were both dead. She knew he had an older brother, a doctor, but he was working somewhere on the other side of the world. Shane had said something about his brother being part of Doctors Without Borders. Other than the fact that he was proud of him and that his brother's name was Alan, she had no other details.

And now, without any warning, she had found Shane just like that. And she had absolutely no idea how she was supposed to act toward him.

It was almost as if she would have been better off left in the dark.

Stop it, Gina silently ordered. *You're acting as if time just stood still and you're the same two people you were back in college. Shane Callaghan is a totally different person than the boy you were in love with ten years ago. And so are you.*

Gina pushed her car key into the ignition and turned it on. The car rumbled to life as she put her foot on the gas. But it went nowhere. Belatedly, she remembered to release the brake and put the car into Reverse. She backed out of the parking space and within seconds, she was on the road.

For all you know, Shane's got a wife and six kids, she told herself. *He certainly didn't act as if he was still in love with you. You're the one with the problem, not him. C'mon, get over yourself.*

She let out a deep breath as she headed for Sylvie Stevens's apartment to share the news about the wedding cake.

This whole ordeal surrounding the creation of the cake might be a little uncomfortable, but it was certainly doable. She would wind up seeing Shane—what? One, maybe two more times and then, presumably, that would be that. No reason to suppose she would have any more contact with him than that.

She didn't want any more contact—did she? Gina silently asked herself as she flew through a yellow light. No, she silently insisted the next moment, she didn't. Definitely not.

And yet…

There was no "yet," she staunchly maintained. She turned the radio up full blast, leaving no room for a miscellaneous thought to push its way forward. She didn't want to think anymore.

Sylvie had made no secret of the fact that she was thrilled and relieved when her new bridesmaid had announced that she had been able to secure Cassidy and that he would indeed be creating the "wedding cake to end all wedding cakes" for Sylvie's big day.

"But he does have one condition before he can get started creating your wedding cake," Gina said before Sylvie could get too carried away heaping a profusion of grateful words on her.

"Anything short of my firstborn is fine with me," Sylvie said enthusiastically. "And even that's negotiable," she added with a laugh.

It never ceased to amaze Gina how obsessed some people could become about something they had essentially talked themselves into thinking that they wanted.

"Nothing that drastic," Gina assured her client. "Sh—Cassidy wants to meet you," she said, correcting herself at the last moment. "He mentioned something about creating a wedding cake being a highly personal process and he needs to get a sense of you before he can even begin the process."

Sylvie seemed to find nothing unusual about that. The young woman was beaming as she said, "That sounds wonderful. Did you get an appointment for us?"

"Us," Gina repeated. "Then your fiancé is coming with you?" she asked hopefully. This was good, Gina thought. Shane had said that he preferred meeting with both parties. This would at least give him less to complain about.

Sylvie's answer unfortunately shot her down. "No," the bride-to-be answered, slightly confused as to how Gina had reached that conclusion. "You are."

"Me?" Gina asked, surprised that the woman had inserted her in her husband's place.

"Of course," Sylvie answered as if this was a no-brainer. "You're the one who was able to talk Cassidy into doing this. Between you and me," Sylvie said, lowering her voice as if she was trying to avoid eavesdroppers, "I've heard he can be temperamental, and I didn't think I had a prayer of his agreeing. But you obviously found a way to get him to agree."

Gina tried one more time to get her client to change her mind. "But wouldn't you rather have your fiancé with you?"

Sylvie laughed lightly. "Jeffery said I could have any kind of wedding I wanted no matter how over-the-top it was. He said I could spend anything I wanted on it. His only condition was that he didn't have to be involved in it beyond showing up on the big day. He said he trusts me," Sylvie declared happily.

This Jeffery sounded almost too good to be true, Gina thought. Either that, or totally uninterested in the proceedings. For Sylvie's sake, she decided to compromise in her thinking. "You're lucky to have someone so easygoing."

"Oh, I know, I know," Sylvie enthused. "So when do we go see the wizard?" she asked.

Gina couldn't help thinking that Sylvie sounded as eager as a young child anticipating her first visit to see the legendary Santa Claus.

She only wished that she felt half as excited as Sylvie was. But then, this wasn't her wedding, it was Sylvie's. Besides, it was hard to be excited when your stomach was tied up in the kind of knots that would have made any Boy Scout proud.

Gina forced a smile to her lips. Hard as it was to project an air of happiness, she had no intention of raining on Sylvie's parade.

"There's a meeting set up for us for ten Wednesday morning," she told the future bride.

"You'll come by and pick me up?" Sylvie asked her, then added as an afterthought, "Seeing as how you know how to get to his shop and all and I don't."

In this day and age, with GPS available on practically every electronic device except for the kitchen stove, that was not really an excuse. The way she saw it, Sylvie was asking her to drive because she just wanted someone to hold her hand before she met the heralded "Cassidy."

Well, that was what she was being paid for, Gina reminded herself.

The big question here was, just who was going to hold *her* hand when she walked into Shane's shop, Gina wondered.

"Of course I'll pick you up, Sylvie. I'll be at your place by nine fifteen Wednesday morning," Gina promised. "That'll give us lots of time in case we run into heavy traffic."

Or maybe, Gina thought as she drove home shortly thereafter, if she was lucky, there'd be an earthquake just before they left. Nothing fancy, just something that would be large enough to shake everything up and prevent her from going.

The next evening, because the prospect of having to see Shane again the next day was making her feel exceptionally restless and more than a little nervous, Gina did what she always did when something was bothering her to this extent.

She called Tiffany.

Two minutes into the conversation, or maybe only ninety seconds, it all came out. She told her sister all about running into Shane the day before and how she had arrived at the shop totally unprepared for the shock of seeing Shane because she thought she was going to be talking to someone named Cassidy.

Rather than being on her side and supportive the way her sister usually was, Tiffany sounded almost delighted to hear about Shane's unexpected materializing in her life. She was extremely eager to hear all the details.

"Shane Callaghan? Really, Gina? After all this time? What's he look like?" Tiffany asked.

Gina frowned. Her usually sedate sister sounded as if she could barely control herself.

"Older," Gina said guardedly, determined to dole out her information if she was forced to share it.

"Older? C'mon, Gina, my German shepherd looks

older than she did yesterday. Use your words," Tiffany told her. "The guy used to be drop-dead gorgeous. Is he fatter, skinnier, dilapidated-looking, bald—what?"

"No," Gina answered slowly, picking out her words as cautiously as if they each had thorns attached. "None of the above."

"He doesn't look any different, then?" Tiffany questioned in disbelief.

"Well, his cheekbones are a little more prominent and he might have gotten a little more distinguished-looking," Gina allowed slowly. And then she stopped. "You're sighing, Tiffany," she accused. "I can hear it. Why are you sighing?"

"I'm just picturing him in my mind, Gee. He was pretty damn near perfect-looking when you two were going together," Tiffany recalled.

"You're exaggerating," Gina said, although she secretly agreed with her sister's assessment.

"No, I'm not. And I'm not the only one who thought he was perfect—inside and out," Tiffany insisted. "Mom was looking into wedding venues for you two minutes after she'd met him."

"Why would she have done that?" Gina asked. This was the first she had heard of this. "We weren't *that* serious in the beginning."

"Mom was," Tiffany told her simply.

Thinking back, maybe her mother was at that, Gina conceded. She knew that her mother had certainly been disappointed when she'd told her that she and Shane had broken up.

"Don't remind me," Gina said with a sigh that came from deep down in her toes. "Look, do me a favor. Don't tell Mom about this, okay? Don't say anything about my running into Shane. *Or* that I have to see him again tomorrow to finalize everything."

"Don't worry. Mom won't hear it from me," Tiffany responded.

Admittedly, Tiffany felt a little guilty about being evasive and about keeping this setup from her sister. But, she silently argued, this was for Gina's own good.

Tiffany consoled herself with the thought that in the long run, Gina would thank her for this even though it was their mother who had gotten everything rolling.

At least, she thought, she could hope so.

Tiffany crossed her fingers as she hung up.

This time, as she drove into the older shopping center, Gina knew just where to pull up and park in order to have better access to Shane's store.

She also knew exactly what was ahead of her.

Which was why her knees felt as if they had been replaced by two vats of whipped butter and her stomach was threatening to separate her from her deliberately light breakfast.

"Is everything all right?" Sylvie asked her when Gina turned off the engine and made no effort to get out.

Still seated in the passenger seat, the excited bride eyed her uncertainly.

Gina slowly took in a deep breath, trying to steady her nerves.

"Everything's fine," Gina quickly assured her client. "I'm just working out some details in my head," she said in order to cover up her preoccupation.

Sylvie didn't appear convinced. "Should I be worried?"

"No, absolutely not," Gina told her with feeling. *Me,*

on the other hand, who knows? "It's right here." Gina pointed out the little shop as she got out of the driver's seat.

Sylvie was immediately beside her, surveying the entire area. "It's perfect," she cried.

"It *is* charming," Gina agreed.

Opening the door and holding it for Sylvie, Gina heard the same quaint bell announce their entrance. But this time, instead of walking into an empty reception area, she found that Shane was waiting for them.

Rather than wearing a spattered apron over his T-shirt and jeans the way he had when she had seen him the other day, Shane was dressed in a suit. No tie, but he didn't need one. He looked like the picture of a rakish businessman.

Was that for his client's benefit, or hers?

Dial it back, Gina. This isn't about you, remember?

Coming to, Gina realized that introductions needed to be made. "Sylvie Stevens, I'd like you to meet—"

"Cassidy," Shane said, stepping forward. Taking Sylvie's hand in his, he kissed it lightly, as if he had grown up somewhere in France or Italy rather than Southern California.

Sylvie giggled at the display of bygone continental manners. When he released her hand, she held it to her as if savoring their fleeting contact.

Belatedly, Sylvie found her tongue. "I can't begin to tell you how grateful I am that you're going to be making my wedding cake."

"*Creating* your wedding cake," Gina interjected, sparing a glance in Shane's direction.

He looked mildly surprised, then smiled as he inclined his head at her.

"Oh, of course," Sylvie agreed. "Right. Creating it,"

she corrected herself. Partially awestruck and totally thrilled, the bride-to-be was having a hard time not tripping over her own tongue.

Shane turned his magnetic blue eyes on the nervous bride. "It'll be my pleasure," he told Sylvie. "Now, why don't we all sit down and you can tell me about yourself and your lucky groom-to-be," he suggested, gesturing toward a small table off to the side.

A table Gina could have sworn was *not* there the day before yesterday.

Like a woman in a trance, Sylvie allowed herself to be led to the table. She was Shane's totally captive audience.

"Ask me anything you want to know," Sylvie said, giving him carte blanche to ask her any intimate detail he wanted to.

Shane waited until the young woman and Gina were both seated, then took a seat himself. After politely offering them coffee or tea, he began asking a series of what initially seemed to be totally unrelated questions.

As Gina listened, she realized that this wasn't just for show. Shane was actually asking Sylvie questions that, once put together, highlighted the personality and preferences of both the bride and, by proxy, her groom.

Was this just to justify what she assumed was going to be a high asking price or did Shane consider all this really a necessary part to fuel his "creative" process?

The Shane she recalled was as far from a huckster as day was from night, but people, she freely admitted, did change. If Shane had changed for the worse, she couldn't help thinking that it might be at least in part her fault. Had she wound up crushing his soul after all or was she just reading much too much into all this?

She listened in silence and found she couldn't really

make a judgment. Shane *sounded* as if he was being genuine, but that might all be just part of his act. She didn't know.

The entire session took about thirty minutes and that was only because Shane didn't rush his client to give him answers. In addition he would interject pleasantries throughout the entire process.

When it was *finally* over, Gina allowed herself one comment. "I had no idea so much went into making the right sort of wedding cake."

Shane's lips curved ever so slightly in a patient smile. "Creating," he reminded her. "Not making."

"Right. Sorry." Her eyes met his. There was that same warm shiver again, working its way up her spine, getting the better of her. "I keep apologizing," she said.

"I noticed. No need to apologize," he replied. His voice grew less formal as he turned to address Sylvie. "I think I have everything I need to at least get started."

"You mean right now?" Sylvie asked, surprised and wide-eyed.

His smile was tolerant. "No, I wasn't being literal. The creating part won't take place until a couple of days before your cake has to become a reality. What I meant was that I have enough information to begin *contemplating* your cake."

"Why don't I give you my number so that if you come up with any further questions, you can just call me and ask," Sylvie said, looking around for a piece of paper and a pen. She was eager to make this as easy as possible for Cassidy.

"No need," he told Sylvie. "I have Gina's number. If I need to ask anything, I'll call her. After all, as your professional bridesmaid, that is her function." His eyes slowly slid over toward Gina. "Am I right?"

It felt as if he had actually touched her, just the way he had back when they were a couple. It took Gina a second to catch her breath. This was *not* going to be smooth sailing.

"Yes," she answered. "You are. Now, if you have nothing else," she said, rising to her feet, "I believe I have a fitting for a bridesmaid dress." She glanced at Sylvie for confirmation.

"Oh right. You do," Sylvie remembered.

She was on her feet as well, shaking Shane's hand and once again restating her gratitude for his making time for her.

He just smiled warmly at the bride.

So why, Gina thought uneasily, did she feel as if he was actually smiling at her—with a promise of things to come?

Chapter Six

This was the part of her job that Gina usually hated: going into the bridal shop and trying on the bridesmaid dress. As a latecomer, she technically had no right to give any input about the dress that had been selected by the bride for her bridal party.

However, coming in as a bridal "troubleshooter," she felt that she did.

As she stood in the store, looking at herself in the mirror, none of that really mattered right now. Maybe it was all relative, considering the emotional ordeal she had just been through, but she thought that the floor-length gown that Sylvie had selected for the five women in her party was rather flattering.

Mint green, high waisted and formfitting, with a side-slit that went just high enough to be inviting but was still rather tasteful, it was a dress Gina would have picked out for herself—if she actually went to places where a dress like this could be deemed appropriate. Which, sadly, she didn't.

"What do you think?" Sylvie asked, watching Gina for a reaction. "It was Jennifer's dress—my bridesmaid who dropped out of the wedding party. She never came in for her last fitting because she was just too despondent after her breakup."

I know how that feels, Gina thought. *Shane didn't break up with you, you broke up with him, remember?* she reminded herself.

She looked herself over one last time. "It's as if it was made for me," she said. Gina turned away from the three-way mirror to look at the woman who was very obviously waiting for her opinion. "It's lovely. You have very good taste," she told Sylvie. "Usually, I find myself searching for a polite way to explain to the prospective bride that if her bridesmaids all resembled escaped trolls, that wasn't going to put her in the kind of spotlight she was hoping for." She turned back for one more glimpse in the mirrors—and smiled. "But this dress is extremely flattering. Any bridesmaid would be thrilled to be in your wedding party."

"Really?" Sylvie asked, absorbing the compliment like a water-deprived thirsty puppy.

Gina's smile widened as she assured the young woman warmly, "Really."

Sylvie caught her off guard by rushing up and embracing her as if she were a long-lost sister. "Thank you!" she cried. "I just *knew* you'd be good luck for me."

Gina felt it was only right if she pointed out one important fact. "You picked these dresses out before you and I even met each other."

Sylvie waved away Gina's words. "It doesn't matter. I just *feel* that you're going to bring me luck. Look how you fit into Jennifer's dress." She said it as if that was an omen. "And you got Cassidy to agree to—*create* the wedding cake," she said, applying the proper amount of emphasis on the process. "And you're getting me another photographer. Have you found one yet?" she asked, suddenly realizing that problem had yet to be resolved.

"I have, and I'll be talking to him once I finish this fitting. And," she added, looking over her shoulder at the way the gown was hugging her curves as it made its way from her hips to her ankles, "in my opinion, this fitting is officially finished."

Having made the declaration, Gina looked around for the seamstress who had come to this session fully equipped with straight pins and two tape measures. She had used none of the tools of her trade because once the gown was on, it became obvious to everyone that alternations were unnecessary.

Spotting the older woman standing over by another display, Gina looked at her with a silent query evident in her expression.

The seamstress, with her short crop of gray hair, looked as if she had been lifted from central casting and told to play the part of a capable seamstress. The woman, Olga, lifted her thin shoulders in a shrug.

Olga's solemn expression didn't change as she said, "I hate to say it, but I cannot improve on perfect."

Gina took one final look at herself. She couldn't help wishing that Shane could suddenly materialize and see her like this.

She sincerely doubted that he ever would. Most likely on the day of the wedding, he would have his assistants bringing in and setting up whatever "masterpiece" he was going to ultimately "create" for the happy couple.

In all probability he wouldn't be anywhere around the vicinity of the reception.

Now that she thought back on it, Gina suddenly remembered that she *had* heard the name Cassidy mentioned before. But there had never been any photographs of him posing with his creations. All she ever saw were isolated cakes taking center stage and a swirly signature superimposed on them.

His signature, she thought.

How had she missed that?

"The dress is rather perfect," Gina said, agreeing with the seamstress.

"I was referring to the way it fit you," the seamstress emphasized. "You have a good body to work with," the woman added matter-of-factly.

Gina smiled. She didn't think of herself in those terms. Most days she just thought of herself as a workhorse, a pawn piece to stick in to take someone else's place and to hopefully help pull off yet another bride's idea of a perfect wedding.

This compliment, coming unbidden from Olga, was like an unexpected bonus. For just a split second, Gina allowed herself to bask in it.

But then Gina reminded herself that she had people to see and things to do—and miles to go before she could sleep, she added whimsically.

"Thank you," she said to the seamstress. "I needed that."

Olga looked at her as if she didn't know what she was talking about. With another careless shrug she went on to say, "I just tell you what I see." She straightened, gathering the tools of her trade to her. "If I am not needed here, I have other work to do for bridesmaids who are not as fortunate as you are," she announced, her eyes antiseptically sweeping over Gina.

With that, the woman withdrew from the room.

Gina noticed that Sylvie was looking at her as if waiting for instructions. Gina felt amused, recalling other brides that were definitely *not* this easy to work with.

"Let me just change back into my clothes and I'll drop you off at your place," she told Sylvie as she made her way into the changing booth.

"When we get to my place you can stay if you like," Sylvie said, almost shyly extending an invitation to her wedding "fixer."

"I'm having the rest of the girls in the bridal party over and it'll give you a chance to meet them."

She thought that was a good idea, but right now, the timing was off. She needed to get the photographer on board. Once she did, that resolved all the outstanding issues for Sylvie—at least for the moment. They still had a long way to go before the wedding.

"Sounds good," Gina answered. "But I'm going to have to take a rain check for now."

"Are you sure?" Sylvie asked. She moved closer to the changing booth, as if proximity would somehow make Gina change her mind.

Having carefully taken off the bridesmaid gown, Gina now threw on her own clothes. Dressed, she proceeded to meticulously hang up the gown in a garment bag and then zipped the bag up.

"I'm sure. I have a photographer to sweet-talk," Gina reminded the bride.

"Oh, that's right. I forgot about that. Good thing you didn't," she added.

"Well, I can't really forget now, can I? That's what you're paying me for." Coming out of the booth and carrying the dress folded in half on her arm, Gina said, "I just had an idea. When does your bridal shower take place?"

Sylvie paused, thinking. By the look on her face, that was obviously something else that the still somewhat harried bride-to-be had forgotten to ask about.

Thinking now, she remembered. "That would be next weekend. You're invited, of course," she quickly told Gina, then murmured, embarrassed, "You must think I'm an airhead."

Gina was quick to squeeze Sylvie's hand and soothingly reassure her. "Absolutely not. Just a woman with a great deal on her mind as the big day draws closer. I'm just here to help you manage all that," she reminded the bride-to-be.

Sylvie smiled her gratitude. "It's a Jack and Jill shower," she added, watching to see if that bothered her new savior in any way.

But Gina welcomed the news. "Good, that'll give me a chance to meet the groom. The reason I asked about the shower is because I thought you might like having professional photographs taken of the event. Unless your fiancé gave you a cut-off point as far as spending money on the wedding went," she quickly added. She knew that this wasn't part of the usual expense associated with a wedding, but she thought that the added event might help get a photographer engaged at this late date. Offering him more money to shoot bridal party photographs could be a further inducement to say yes.

"No, no limits," Sylvie told her. "Jeffery just wants me happy. And as for your suggestion, I think it's wonderful." Her smile grew with each word she uttered. "I'd love to have professional photographs taken of the party." She impulsively hugged Gina again. "You have just the *best* ideas," she declared with enthusiasm.

"I just want to make this the best wedding possible for you," Gina told her.

An almost starry look entered Sylvie's eyes. "It really is starting to look that way, isn't it?" she said happily.

"Absolutely."

Gina dropped Sylvie off at her apartment.

The meeting with the photographer she had selected didn't turn out the way she had hoped. Like the photographer before him, the photographer she had wanted to hire for this wedding turned out to have a conflict. He had regretfully told her that he wasn't available.

Disappointed but undaunted because she did have several other photographers to check out, Gina drove home and spent her evening poring over their websites. Eventually narrowing her search down to two candidates, she jotted both names down along with their accompanying phone numbers.

She promised herself she'd call the one at the top of the list first thing in the morning.

Worn out, she finally went to bed.

Exhausted, Gina fell asleep before her head even hit the pillow. And then proceeded to have one dream after another, each one involving Shane in some way.

The dreams, some fragments, some feeling as if they were practically feature-length movies, all involved a wealth of warm emotions that insisted on infiltrating her. All through the night Gina found herself vividly reminded of the way she had felt when she and Shane had been going together.

That, in turn, reminded her just how much she had regretted turning Shane down almost from the very moment that she had. Because once her fears had subsided, allowing her to think logically again, she realized that she *did* love Shane and she wanted nothing more than to face forever with him.

But by then it was too late.

Shane had disappeared as if he had existed only in her mind.

The way he did now in the dreams that kept assaulting her brain.

Gina couldn't help thinking that one stupid wrong move had cost her everything.

Regret left a horrible, bitter taste in her mouth.

"Maybe this is our second chance. We can do this over again." Gina could have sworn she heard Shane whispering that to her.

And then suddenly, he was there, right behind her. Wrapping his arms around her and making her feel safe and protected.

The way, she recalled, that she used to.

She was vividly aware of turning around in the shelter of his arms. Aware of her heart pounding wildly as he slowly began to lower his mouth to hers.

Aware of wanting Shane more than she wanted anything else in this life.

She felt whole.

She felt—

With a start, Gina jerked upright in her bed, her heart

pounding double time, threatening to crack right through her ribs.

The room—her bedroom—was still dark with only whispers of an approaching dawn beginning to infiltrate the darkness.

She was alone.

Alone just as she had been ever since she had allowed fear to speak for her all those years ago, thereby eliminating the best thing in her life.

She had no one to blame for this but herself, she thought.

Gina sat up straighter, dragging a hand through her hair. She was trying desperately to get her brain into focus.

C'mon, Gina. Get with it!

There was no sense in going over the same old thoughts she'd had time and again over these last ten years. This was old ground and if she covered it again, nothing new would come of it. She had a job to do, she reminded herself. Sylvie was paying her to make sure she took care of all things associated with the wedding. She certainly wasn't paying her to mourn over her own stupidity.

Kicking her covers aside, Gina got up and made her way into the bathroom.

Maybe a shower would do the trick and bring her around.

She looked like hell, Gina thought, catching a glimpse of her reflection in the bathroom mirror.

"Time to do a little damage control and get back into the game," she ordered her reflection.

This was her eternal penance, Gina thought as she stepped into the shower and turned on the water.

Cold water hit her body with the force of a thousand needles. It made her focus.

She had callously ruined her own prospects and for that she was going to spend the rest of her life making sure that other women got the fairy-tale wedding she had turned her back on.

Gina met with the photographer she had put in first place on her list after her initial candidate said he wasn't available. Happily, this new candidate *was* free for not just the day of the wedding, but he was also available for the bridal shower, as well.

Closing the deal, Gina left the photographer's studio with a firm commitment—and with a brand-new idea.

She realized that part of the reason she was having dreams about Shane was because she had been racking her brain trying to come up with a legitimate reason to go see him again.

She couldn't just go back and apologize to him again about the way she had turned down his proposal. Thinking it over now, that would just seem like she was rubbing salt into his wound. Besides, if she apologized again, in all likelihood, he would just shut her out. She didn't want to grovel. Groveling sent the wrong message to the man, not to mention that it put her in a position of weakness. That was *not* the image she wanted to project, nor did she think that Shane would look at her favorably if that was the way she came across.

That was if he had any sort of a favorable view of her left, she amended.

What this needed, what they *both* needed, was a fresh start, a clean slate. The one thing they still had in common was confections. Sylvie was having a bridal shower and a bridal shower needed refreshments. From everything she had read about Cakes Created by Cassidy he didn't just make wedding cakes. He could make—*create*, she corrected herself—all sorts of different kinds of pastries.

Since he had agreed to do Sylvie's wedding cake, maybe she could prevail on him to handle her bridal shower, as well.

And if he turned the request down, citing how "busy" he was, well at least she would have gotten another opportunity to see him again. And maybe seeing her a few times would hopefully wear him down, make him remember just what it was that had attracted him to her in the first place.

Maybe it would even make him decide that what they'd had was worth giving a second chance.

One step at a time, Gina, she cautioned, trying not to get ahead of herself.

Even so, she did a quick U-turn and instead of going to Shane's shop, she went home first. Although she always dressed nicely, she wanted to put on something *extra*nice. While she was at it, she also wound up freshening up her makeup.

After checking herself over several times and deciding that if she did anything more elaborate, it would wind up looking like overkill, Gina drove to Shane's shop at the shopping center.

Although the distance between her apartment and the shopping center wasn't very far, her palms were damp by the time she pulled her vehicle up in front of his show window.

This was crazy. She hadn't been this nervous even on her first date with Shane.

But there was a lot more riding on this now, she thought.

Turning off the car engine, Gina gave herself one final pep talk and got out of the car.

The same tinkling sound announced her entrance this time as it had the other two times.

The reception area was empty.

A wave of déjà vu washed over her. And then, suddenly, she heard the sound of laughter. Gleeful childish laughter.

The next moment, the door leading from the back area opened and a little girl of about four or five came dashing into the reception area.

The little girl was holding what looked like a measuring spoon gripped tightly in her hand and there were traces of whipped cream outlining her lower lip. There was also some whipped cream on her right cheek.

She stopped in her tracks when she saw Gina. But instead of being afraid, the little girl looked exceptionally comfortable and secure. She offered her a huge smile.

"Hello," Gina said, her interest definitely engaged. "And whose little girl are you?"

"His," the girl answered, pointing just as Shane walked in behind her.

Chapter Seven

Shane quickly crossed the room and made his way over to the little girl. Placing one hand on her shoulder, he made eye contact with her.

"Ellie, you know what I told you about talking to strangers," Shane told her sternly.

But the little girl didn't seem to be intimidated. "You said not to," she answered.

Ellie was usually either in preschool or with the woman he employed as a part-time nanny. But there was no preschool for her today and Barbara, Ellie's nanny, had a doctor's appointment so he had brought Ellie to work with him. It wasn't really a hardship. The little girl loved the shop and moved through it as if it was her own private playground.

At times Ellie could be a little too brave and that concerned him. While Shane didn't want her to grow up frightened, he also didn't want to have to worry about Ellie going off with the first stranger who was nice to her. He was beginning to learn that this wasn't an easy thing to pull off.

Continuing to make eye contact with Ellie, Shane replied, "Exactly."

Ellie peered around him at Gina. "But she looks friendly," the little girl argued in her own defense.

Turning, Shane spared a glance at Gina. "Looks," he said cryptically, "can be deceiving."

"What's de-de-deceiving?" Ellie asked, pleased with herself for getting the word right after two attempts.

"That's when somebody tries to fool you."

It wasn't Shane who answered her. It was Gina. Shane's words had cut into her like a sharp, jagged knife. She truly wished that there was some way she could make what had happened between them up to him, to prove to him how very sorry she was.

But then he really didn't need her to do that, she thought. Shane had obviously moved on. He had a daughter. He might have other children, as well. Now that she looked at the little girl's face, she could easily see the resemblance. The dirty blond hair, the bright blue eyes, and especially when Ellie smiled. That was all Shane.

Without realizing it, Gina glanced down at his left hand. There was still no ring there, but that didn't mean anything. Some men didn't wear wedding rings. Others took theirs off when they worked because they didn't want to risk getting the ring caught on machinery. In this case, that could include appliances.

Searching for neutral ground, Gina smiled at Shane and said, "She's very cute."

Though he doted on Ellie, he pretended to shrug indifferently. "She has her moments," he replied.

He was still pretending to be stern for Ellie's sake. But he couldn't quite pull that off, not when it came to Ellie. Being the tough disciplinarian never really suited him.

He ruffled Ellie's blond curls and she made a face as she ducked her head away.

"You're messing it up," Ellie complained. She raised her hands and with careful movement, she smoothed down her hair.

Gina couldn't help but laugh. "She's all girl, all right," she said to Shane.

Gina wasn't telling him anything he didn't already know. His eyes narrowed a little as he turned to look at Gina. He hadn't been expecting her. It bothered him that she kept catching him off guard.

"She is that," he agreed. "But you didn't come here just to evaluate Ellie." Up until a few minutes ago, she hadn't even known about the little girl's existence, he thought. "What are you doing here?" he asked Gina bluntly.

Making a fool of myself, Gina thought, although she forced a neutral smile to her lips. *Okay, here goes nothing.*

"You know that woman you agreed to make that wedding cake for? Sylvie Stevens," she said in case Shane didn't remember who she was talking about.

"Yes?" he prompted, waiting for her to get to the point.

He deliberately kept any and all emotions out of his voice. As a result, it sounded almost icy cold. Part of the reason for that was because he didn't want her realizing that he hadn't agreed to make the cake for this Sylvie person, he had agreed to make it for her.

Because, despite everything she had put him through, he wanted an excuse to see her again.

Gina cleared her throat and pressed on. "Well, I know this is probably asking for a lot, but she's having a bridal shower this weekend—"

"Doesn't the lady take showers every day?" Ellie asked, curious.

Grateful for the distraction, Gina looked at the little girl. "It's not that kind of a shower, honey. That's what they call a party for a bride before she gets married," she explained.

"Then she doesn't have to get wet?" Ellie asked. She screwed up her face, doing her best to understand.

Knowing how involved things could get when explaining them to Ellie, Shane tactfully suggested, "Ellie, why don't you go in the back and tell one of my assistants that you need someone to play with you?"

Thinking he was shooing the little girl out for her benefit, Gina vetoed the idea. "That's okay," she told Shane and then crouched down to the little girl's level. "I don't mind explaining things. Bridal shower is really a silly name for it," she agreed with Ellie. "I think they call it that because people come to the party and they shower the bride with presents. That means they give the bride presents," she clarified just in case Ellie still didn't understand.

But Ellie understood just fine. Her sky-blue eyes opened wide as the information penetrated.

"Really?" she asked gleefully, clapping her hands together. Her head swirled toward Shane. "Can I have a bridal shower?"

"Not for a long, long time," Gina told her. "Someone has to ask you to marry them first."

"How do I get them to do that?" Ellie asked earnestly.

Bad example to use, Gina realized. She could literally *feel* Shane looking at her. Was he waiting to hear what she was going to say in response, or was he just going to shoot her down without bothering to listen to her say anything else?

But his silence dragged out so she gave Ellie an answer.

"Well, if you're very lucky, you meet a nice boy and the two of you fall in love. After a while, he asks you to marry him and then—"

"Do I hafta wait for the boy to ask me?" Ellie asked, interrupting impatiently. "Can't I ask him to marry me?"

That caught Gina by surprise. It took her a moment to answer. "You can," she told the girl.

"Good, 'cause I don't like to wait," Ellie informed her.

"Well, I'm sorry, kiddo, but you're going to have to wait awhile longer," Shane told the girl. He didn't want any ideas put into that blond little head. "At least thirty years. Maybe more. Now go in the back and play like I told you," he instructed. Seeing Ellie interacting with Gina took him to places he didn't want to go. There was no sense in allowing that to happen.

Ellie made a face, but even at her tender young age, she seemed instinctively to know when not to push. "Oh, okay."

Gina caught herself looking after the little girl almost yearningly as Ellie all but skipped out of the room.

If things had turned out differently—if she hadn't been such a coward, she upbraided herself—that little girl could have been hers. Hers and Shane's.

"She looks like she has a lot of energy," she commented.

"You don't know the half of it," Shane answered. "It's nonstop all day long."

Myriad questions filled Gina's head, questions she couldn't risk asking right now. Things were still very raw and tenuous between them. If she said or asked the wrong thing, she was afraid that Shane would change his mind and back out of making the wedding cake for Sylvie. She couldn't afford to do that to her client just because her curiosity was aroused.

Besides, maybe she didn't really want to hear about Shane and Ellie's mother. She might not be able to handle it. It was one thing to tell herself that she knew Shane had moved on, it was totally another to actually see living proof that he had.

As it was, she was trying to block the sudden ache she felt in the pit of her stomach.

"You said something about a bridal shower?" Shane prompted, the sound of his voice breaking the awkward silence growing between them.

"Yes, I did," she said, forcing herself to come around. "I was wondering if you could possibly see your way to providing some of your pastries for the bridal shower. Nothing unique," she quickly qualified, not wanting to put any undue pressure on him—or give him a reason to turn her down.

"If you don't want anything unique, why don't you just go to your local Costco and get the pastries there?" Shane asked.

She wasn't doing this right, Gina thought. She tried again. "Okay, maybe we do want something unique," she qualified.

And then, because she felt this wasn't going well, Gina stopped and took a deep breath. She couldn't keep tap-dancing around the very large elephant in the room like this any longer. It was obvious that ignoring it wasn't working. She needed to get it out of the way if she had any hopes of making progress.

"All right," she said, bracing herself, "you want the truth?"

Shane's eyes held hers prisoner. "That would be a unique experience," Shane agreed. "Go ahead, tell me the truth," he challenged.

"The truth is I was trying to find an excuse to see you again. The bridal shower seemed like the right way to go." Gina wanted to look away, but she knew that would be a mistake. She needed to tell him this to his face, not address his shadow. "I thought that maybe the more we saw each other, the less awkward it would be."

The silence threatened to engulf them. And then he said, "I guess you were wrong."

Her heart sank. "I guess I was." Gina gathered her courage together. "But I'd just like to go on record to tell you that I'm sorry. That I behaved like an idiot that day you proposed to me because I was afraid of having anything change between us. I thought if we changed one thing, the magic we had would disappear. I realized how dumb that was practically from the moment I pushed you away.

"And I did try to go back and apologize," she stressed, "but by then you'd taken off somewhere. I asked everyone who was still there and no one knew where you were." Her voice throbbed with sincerity. "I tried everything. Your social footprint disappeared completely. But I kept trying anyway. After a year, I finally realized that you didn't want to be found." She pressed her lips together. "I just wanted you to know that," she told Shane.

It was hard to talk when she could feel tears gathering in her throat. But somehow, she had managed.

With that, Gina turned away from him. She was almost at the door, her hand on the doorknob when she heard Shane ask, "You looked for me for a whole year?"

She tried but she couldn't read his tone. Was Shane mocking her or did he finally believe her? She couldn't tell.

Gina turned around to look at him. "I did. I tried to find your friends but the ones who were still around hadn't seen or heard from you. They were just as surprised as I was that you'd vanished." She pressed her lips together, debating telling him this, then decided there was no point in hiding it. "I even filed a missing person's report."

He stared at her, stunned. "You did what? With the police?" he asked incredulously.

She couldn't tell if he was angry or not, but now that she'd said it, she had to give him the details. "I was afraid something had happened to you. I knew I had hurt you, but I didn't think you would just disappear like that without telling anyone. That's why I filed the report. But the police couldn't find you either," she said.

She shrugged helplessly. "Eventually, I suppose the missing person's report was filed with all the other unsolved cases and went into missing person's limbo." She took another deep breath, searching his face, waiting for an explanation for his disappearance.

He didn't say anything.

She gathered up her courage again. "I know that you

don't owe me any explanations, but where were you all that time?"

His eyes met hers. He could still read her, he thought. That was oddly comforting. "You were really worried?"

"I thought if something hadn't happened to you, then maybe you had done something to yourself and that it was all my fault," she said, letting out a shaky breath. She hadn't admitted that to anyone before. It felt good to finally get it out. "You have no idea what went on in my head."

"I guess I didn't," he admitted. "After you turned me down, I couldn't deal with it. I just wanted to get away, so I left. Alan told me that he welcomed any help I could offer. He was a doctor volunteering his services in the poorest region in Uganda," Shane explained. "There was nothing keeping me here any longer so I went."

She should have known. Shane had found something good to do with his life, something that hadn't even oc-curred to her.

"And did what?" she asked, hungry for any details he could spare her.

He shrugged. "Anything and everything. I cleaned wounds, carried water, drove hundreds of miles for much-needed supplies when they became available. I did whatever my brother's small band of selfless doc-tors and nurses needed. I guess you could say I was their Man Friday," he added with a touch of self-deprecating humor.

Well, that explained why she couldn't find him. But not how he got to his present position. "So how did you get from there to being a renowned pastry chef?" she asked in wonder.

He wasn't about to get into that right now. He couldn't.

"It's a long story," he told her. "And I have a full schedule."

She nodded. She hadn't expected him to tell her as much as he had.

"Right. I won't keep you," Gina told him, pushing her purse's strap up her shoulder.

She was almost out the door again when she heard him ask, "When's the bridal shower again?"

She swung around, grateful for the chance to exchange a few more words with him. "This coming Sunday. At two. It's local," she added, then crossed her fingers as she told him, "You're welcome to come."

"To a bridal shower?" he questioned, bemused.

"It's a Jack and Jill shower," she said. Thinking he might not know the term, she started to explain. "That's when—"

"I know what that is," Shane said, cutting her short. "But I'll pass. On the shower, not on bringing the pastries," he clarified.

At least that was something, she thought. "Really? Sylvie will be thrilled. And I was serious about the invitation," she reiterated, giving it another shot. She wanted them to at least be friends. "You could bring your wife."

That caught him totally off guard. "My what?"

"Your wife," she repeated. "The more the merrier." Did that sound as trite to him as it did in her head? she wondered.

Rather than answering, he asked his own question. "What makes you think I have a wife?"

"Ex-wife?" Gina asked. Had she made a mistake, or didn't he want to talk about his situation? When he just went on looking at her, she felt she had to explain why she had assumed he was married. "Isn't Ellie your daughter?"

"Look, I've got a full schedule—" he began, attempting to dismiss this woman who had materialized out of his past.

"I know," she assured him quickly. "I didn't mean to keep you, I just—"

A quick getaway was impossible with Gina. He should have remembered that. "You still don't let me talk, do you?" he marveled. "I was going to say that I have a busy schedule, but if you'd like to get a cup of coffee with me say about six, maybe we can talk then."

Talk? He wanted to talk. Hope sprang up in her chest. Maybe they *could* be friends after all. She needed to rearrange a couple of things to make the meeting, but there was no way she was going to stand him up.

"I'll be here at six," she told him.

"Not here," Shane told her. "Why don't you meet me at the coffee shop at the other end of the shopping center. Molly's," he told her in case Gina was unaware of the place.

"Molly's at six. Got it. I'll be there," Gina promised. She had an urge to hug him, but she refrained. She didn't want to scare him off.

She walked out of the small shop feeling happier than she remembered feeling in a long time. She had no delusions that having coffee with Shane would lead to anything else. It wasn't going to change anything. The man was married or at the very least had been involved with Ellie's mother and still might be. Knowing his personality, she didn't think that there was any chance that she would be able to suddenly pick up with him after all these years, especially if there was someone else in

the picture. And she didn't want to ruin whatever it was
that he had going on.

She had missed her chance and she had to make her
peace with that all over again. But she did want the man
to be happy. That hadn't changed.

"I have wonderful news," she told Sylvie, calling her
client once she got into her car. "I talked to…Cassidy,"
she said, stopping herself from referring to him as Shane.
"And he said that he would be happy to make the pastry
refreshments for your bridal shower."

"Oh, Gina, you really are a miracle worker!" Sylvie
gushed.

"No, not really." She didn't want to take any credit
that wasn't due to her. "He wasn't all that hard to convince. Now that he's handling your wedding cake, I think
he feels as if he has a stake in your wedding, as well."

"He wouldn't be doing the wedding cake if it wasn't
for you. I'm going to tell all my friends about you—some
of them aren't married yet," she added. "With any luck,
you'll be getting so much business coming your way,
you won't have time to breathe."

"Sounds good to me," Gina said.

This way, if she'd be busy she wouldn't have time to
think about the one who got away and what a mistake
she'd made pushing him out of her life.

Chapter Eight

Gina shifted in her seat and looked down at her watch again. If she didn't know that it was impossible, she would have said that her watch had stopped. But it certainly felt that way because the hands on her wristwatch hadn't moved since the last time she had looked at it.

Or the time before that.

She had made sure that she'd gotten here at five fifty, arriving ten minutes earlier than the time they had agreed upon. It wasn't her habit to arrive early, but she didn't want to take a chance on finding herself stalled in traffic. Granted this wasn't LA with its soul-sucking traffic jams, but Orange County wasn't exactly smooth sailing during rush hour, which wasn't an hour but more like three. Or four.

The last thing she wanted was to have Shane walk into the coffee shop at six and not find her there. With

her luck, he would wind up jumping to the very logical conclusion that she had decided not to come and see
him after all.

He didn't come in at six.

She had been sitting here at this table for two for almost thirty minutes now, Gina thought, staring at the
analog numbers that were flashing across her watch.
What if *he* wasn't coming? What if Shane had thought
better of having her meet him for coffee and had just
decided not to show up?

How long did she have to sit here before she finally
gave up?

There were a million reasons why he wouldn't show
up. But none that she could come up with that would
keep him from calling and letting her know that he
wasn't coming.

Maybe it was just a simple matter of getting even,
her mind whispered.

No, Shane wasn't like that, she argued the next moment.

She was thinking of the *old* Shane, Gina reminded
herself. What did she know about what the new Shane
was like?

Maybe this *was* payback. Maybe he wanted to pay
her back for breaking his heart the way she had when
she had so abruptly and thoughtlessly turned him down.

She saw the server behind the counter who had made
her coffee drink looking at her with pity in her eyes. She
was so obviously waiting for someone.

What was she doing here anyway? Gina silently demanded. If she had a lick of sense left, she'd get up
and walk out instead of sitting here like some kind of a
mindless robot.

But despite her silent pep talk, she just couldn't get herself to get up and leave, couldn't get herself to give up the hope that Shane was just running late. After all, he *had* told her that he had a busy schedule.

In addition to his work, there was that little girl of his. What if the reason he was late had something to do with her?

So she remained sitting at the table, silently making up excuses for Shane and all but jumping out of her skin every time the entrance door opened. And each time it did, she could feel her heart sinking, dropping down into her stomach with a thud because it wasn't Shane.

This couldn't go on indefinitely, she told herself. She could only nurse her overpriced coffee for so long. It was almost all gone and she couldn't just continue sitting here once it was finished. She knew that the store had a strict policy about loitering. She supposed she could always order another container, but she had never developed a taste for these high-caloric drinks.

And then, at six forty-two when she had finally convinced herself to get up and leave the shop, the front door opened and this time it wasn't some stranger coming in. It was Shane.

Maybe it had something to do with the fact that she had consumed a large container of designer coffee while she'd waited, but her mouth suddenly went incredibly dry. So dry that she was worried her tongue was hermetically sealed to the roof of her mouth.

She raised her hand halfway so he could see where she was, although the place wasn't *that* big.

He'd quickly scanned the area. Seeing Gina, Shane crossed to her small table over in the corner. He nodded at her and spared her the barest hint of a smile.

"Sorry I'm late," he told her.

She was about to say something flippant about just having gotten there herself, but she decided against it. She didn't want to start off their renewed relationship with a lie.

So instead Gina merely nodded at his apology. "I'm sure you have your reasons for being late, and besides," she stressed, "this isn't anything formal. It's just two old friends getting together for coffee." She watched his face to see if he agreed with her, but she couldn't read his expression.

"Is that what you think?" he asked her. It wasn't a challenge, it was a simple question. "That we're old friends?"

Gina felt as if she was trying to make her way across a tightrope. Determined, she pushed on. "I think we could be. We were once," she reminded him.

"Were we?" Shane questioned. And then, with a shrug, he changed the subject. "I'd better go get some coffee. They don't like people just sitting around without buying anything."

With that, Shane got up and walked over to the counter. He placed his order, then, to her surprise, he came back to the table to wait for that order to be filled. She would have thought that he'd use the excuse of waiting for his drink to continue standing by the counter rather than to sit with her.

Maybe there *was* hope, she thought.

Which was why she said, "We were," as Shane sat back down.

He looked at her blankly. She realized that he had lost the thread of their conversation—or was pretending he had.

"We were what?" Shane asked.

"Friends. You asked if we were friends just before you went to place your order. I'm answering your question. We were." Her voice grew more confident as she went on to make her point. "We were friends before anything ever developed between us."

This was killing her, this limbo she suddenly found herself lost in. Did he forgive her? Hate her? She couldn't tell and the not knowing was seriously adding to this agitated state she felt growing within her. One minute she was hopeful, the next she was courting despondency.

"Why did you ask me here?" she asked. She thought she had convinced herself that just being able to see him was good enough, but it wasn't. Not when she wasn't sure where she stood with Shane.

He was quiet for a moment, as if deciding whether to answer her or not. And then he asked, "Did you really file a missing person's report on me?"

At least this she could address. "Yes, I did. I was desperate and I'd run out of ideas on how to find you. You'd just packed up and disappeared," she reminded him. "It was like you didn't exist, like I had just conjured you up in my mind. Except that I hadn't."

"And you felt what, guilty?" Shane guessed, his eyes intently on her.

The server at the counter called out his name and he rose. "Hold that thought," Shane told her as he went to get his drink.

When he returned, Gina answered his question. "Guilty, scared, angry. You name it, I felt it," she said honestly. "It was like everything suddenly stopped and wouldn't start up again until I could find out what happened to you."

"But you just said you didn't find out," he reminded Gina.

"No," she agreed. "I didn't. One day I realized that my living in limbo was getting to my mother and the rest of my family, so I forced myself to snap out of it." She sighed. None of this had been easy at the time. "I pulled myself together, got a job, then got another job until I finally decided that what I had studied in school really wasn't me. None of that was me. So I found something else to do with my life."

He took a sip of his drink before saying anything. When he did, it wasn't exactly a revelation. "And you became a professional bridesmaid."

She couldn't tell if he was mocking her choice or if he was surprised by it. In either case, taking offense wouldn't get her anywhere, so she decided to poke fun at herself instead.

"You know the old saying. Those who can, do, those who can't, teach," she told him.

He nodded. And then he took her completely by surprise as he told her, "I guess I wanted to see you so I could apologize."

She weighed her words carefully, knowing that if she responded the wrong way, she would succeed only in chasing him away. But she did need to know why he thought he needed to apologize to her.

"For?"

"For disappearing without telling you where I was going." He understood now that it must have been hard for her to deal with. "In my defense, I didn't think you much cared."

"Of course I cared." It was an effort to keep her voice down, but what Shane had just said was completely ridiculous. "Just because I didn't want to get married the second we were out of school didn't mean I didn't care, that I didn't love you." For the first time, she looked directly into his eyes, searching for the man she had loved. How could he have doubted that even for a second? "The exact opposite was true."

"And you decided to show me how much you loved me by turning me down," he told her. He was highly skeptical of her protest.

"I didn't turn you down, not really. Not in the forever sense." She could see he didn't believe her. "I was stalling," she explained.

His brow furrowed as he tried to make sense out of what she was saying. Despite the number she had done on his heart and his ego, heaven help him but he did still love her.

"Stalling?" he questioned.

"I was afraid that if we changed the dynamic we were in, you'd eventually realize that you'd made a mistake." She could tell by the look on his face that he didn't understand, but she went on. "That you'd realize that you really didn't want to be married to me and then I'd lose you. I just wanted to keep everything the way it was a little longer."

"What kind of twisted logic is that?" he asked, shaking his head at what he felt was the sheer mind-boggling stupidity of it all.

"My logic," she said simply. "Don't forget, I was twenty-two, fresh out of college with no real-life experience."

Shane gazed into his cup and at the fading foam for

what seemed like an inordinate amount of time. And then he finally looked up at her.

He supposed, seeing it from her point of view, he could sort of understand what she was saying. But she should have come to him with that, not made him feel as if she was throwing cold water on his plans.

They had both made mistakes. And their lives had changed because of it.

"In hindsight, maybe I should have left you a note," he conceded. "But I was so hurt by your flat-out refusal that I just wanted to get away from the scene of my disaster. I wanted to put as much distance between us as possible." An ironic smile curved his mouth. "And then my brother showed up on my doorstep. He'd come for my graduation."

"I don't remember meeting your brother at graduation," Gina said.

"That's because Alan's flight got delayed. He wound up arriving two days late—just after you had turned me down."

Gina winced. With all her heart, she wished she could be able to relive that day. She'd do it all differently now.

"Alan saw something was wrong. Instead of giving me a pep talk, he offered me a way to see beyond my own small world. He asked if I wanted to come back with him to Uganda and help people who really needed help, people who had nothing. Before I knew it, I said yes and I was on a plane, heading for Uganda."

"You could have written," Gina told him.

Her voice wasn't accusing, she was just pointing out the fact that he could have found a way to get in contact with her and let her know what he was doing. He didn't even have to call. Just a simple note would have been enough. A simple note would have spared her a world of grief.

But then, she had also caused him grief, Gina reminded herself. So maybe in his mind, that made them even.

"I could have," Shane acknowledged, and looking back, he knew he should have. But at the time, he wasn't thinking clearly. "But I was angry and hurt and thought you didn't care. And then, once I got there, I was just too caught up in what needed doing to take the time to write. Life in that country is totally different than what we're used to over here. I found I had no time to think about myself. Or you."

He paused for a moment and looked at her. "I guess that was the whole point, not to think about you."

His words reverberated within her. Though she wanted to fault Shane, she really couldn't. Gina now understood why he had felt the way he had.

There was something about his story that didn't quite add up as far as she was concerned. "How long have you been back?"

"Three years," he answered.

And if she was any judge of ages, his daughter was four. Which meant that he had gotten together with the girl's mother almost five years ago. Not exactly the solitary life he was painting.

"Well, it seems like you must have had time to think about someone," Gina said.

He finished the last of his coffee and set down the container. "I'm not sure what you're getting at."

"Ellie's mother," Gina answered. She deliberately kept any accusation out of her voice. But for her own sake, she needed to get this straightened out. "You must have found time for her. Was Ellie's mother a nurse?" Gina was trying to piece together his life as best she could. Shane wasn't exactly a font of information.

"Yes," he replied, recalling the woman. "Ellie's mother was a nurse."

It was like pulling words out of his throat, she thought impatiently. "And did she come here with you when you left Uganda?"

"No." The word rang with finality. And then he told her, "Ellie's mother is dead."

Gina was instantly filled with regret. Here she was, being jealous and Shane was dealing with a tragedy. "Oh, I'm so sorry, Shane. What happened?" The moment she asked, she realized how intrusive her question was. "You don't have to tell me if you don't want to, but no matter what you think of me, I'm here for you if you want to talk. You have to believe me when I tell you that I have always wanted you to be happy. You deserve to be happy."

Gina paused, but he wasn't saying anything. Shane wasn't answering her questions or commenting on anything she'd just said. Had he decided to give her the silent treatment?

"Is that why you're back?" she pressed. "To try to make sure that you give your daughter a better life over here?"

Shane debated just letting her go on thinking that, but now that they were finally attempting to clear the air, he couldn't allow the lie to continue. It wouldn't be fair to his brother.

"Ellie's not my daughter," he told her.

She looked at him, stunned. Why was he saying that? "Sure she is," she told him. Maybe she'd believe what he was saying if the little girl didn't have all his features. "Ellie looks just like you."

"That might be," he allowed. "But she's not my daughter. Ellie's my niece."

Now Gina was really stunned. "She's your what?"

"My niece," Shane repeated. "She's my brother's daughter."

It still wasn't making any sense to her. "And your brother's all right with you bringing Ellie back to the States?"

Shane laughed dryly. It surprised him that Gina was so concerned about his brother, seeing as how she hadn't even met Alan. "He probably would be if he had a say in anything. But he's not saying anything these days. Alan's been dead for three years." He saw the stunned sympathy on Gina's face and just for a moment he felt close to her the way he had all those years ago. But then that feeling faded. "He and his wife were both killed on their way to bring medicine to some of the villagers."

"Car accident?" she asked in a hushed voice.

He shook his head. "No, it was as a result of an uprising. The locals were challenging the people currently in power. As it turned out, Alan and his wife, Mandy, were caught in the crossfire. The old jeep they were driving exploded when a stray bullet hit the gas tank." He walled himself off from the details he was telling her. He couldn't function otherwise. "I buried their charred bodies, grabbed Ellie and got on the first plane back to the States.

"I was lucky because our parents had set up a large trust fund for both of us. When I came back, I used my share to help set up my business and finance it."

"Cake creating?" she questioned. She was still having a hard time wrapping her head around that. "How did you come up with that?"

"I found out I had a knack for baking while I was over there with Alan and his wife. The locals only thought of food as a way to survive. Cakes and pastries were unimaginable treats for them. My first efforts weren't too great," he recalled with a smile. "But I got better at it. And I got hooked on the mesmerized expressions on their faces when they devoured what I'd baked for them. So whenever I could—and we had the supplies—I'd bake something. I found that it helped fulfill me.

"When I came back with Ellie, I knew I needed something that would make me feel whole again. My own business where I could keep her around so that she wouldn't feel abandoned. After all, she'd lost her parents when she was only a little more than a year old and I was the only family she had. Her mother, Mandy, had been an orphan," he explained. "It was one of the things that she and my brother bonded over. That and their desire to help people," he added with pride.

"Anyway, creating cakes seemed like the perfect solution to me as far as having my own business went," he concluded. "Any more questions?" he asked.

Gina shook her head. For once in her life, she found herself utterly speechless.

Chapter Nine

Given Gina's personality, Shane was surprised when she didn't say anything in response. "Did I overwhelm you?"

Managing to collect herself, Gina said, "No. It's just a lot to process." She let out a long breath. "But you did answer all my questions." She thought about everything he had just told her. "You do have a lot going on," she freely acknowledged. "What with running your own business and being a single parent—did I get that right? You *are* a single parent?" she asked, having really no idea how he saw himself in this situation.

Did Ellie think he was her father, or had he told the little girl that he was her uncle? Gina didn't want to take a chance on messing anything up for him by making the wrong reference around the little girl.

"Single uncle," Shane corrected. "Ellie knows I'm her

uncle. I've shown her pictures of her dad and her mother ever since she was old enough to recognize faces. She knows all about how she came to live with me here in Southern California."

That must have been hard for him in many ways, Gina thought. It had to be painful talking about his late brother's death and yet he'd had to have kept it simple enough for his niece to understand.

"That's very progressive of you," Gina told him.

Shane merely shrugged. For him there had been no other option. "Lies have a way of bogging you down. It's much easier in the long run to stick with the truth. And if that was your subtle way of asking me if there's someone currently in my life over three feet tall," he said with just a hint of a smile, "there isn't. Between raising Ellie and running my business, there's just no time for anything else."

After saying that, Shane rose to his feet. He'd done what he came to do. He'd wanted to apologize to Gina for being so cold and abrupt with her earlier. Now that he had, it was time to leave.

Gina took the hint and got up from the table. Grateful that Shane had finally opened up a little to her, she didn't want this to be the last time that they talked like this. Yes, he was taking care of the pastries for Sylvie's shower and the cake for her client's wedding, but she really didn't want that to be the end of it. There had to be a way for them to stay in touch.

She thought of the little girl he was raising. If he was anything like some of her friends, half the time he probably had no idea what he was doing. Maybe he could use a little supportive help. After all, he had said that there was no other family for him to turn to for help or emotional support.

"Listen, I enjoyed clearing the air like this," Gina began. Shane nodded and turned to walk out. She put her hand on his arm to stop him for a second longer. "If you find that you ever do need help with Ellie, you have my number. Don't hesitate to call me. I'm really good with kids."

Shane didn't respond. He walked with Gina to the shop's entrance, then held the door open for her.

"I thought you were so busy," he finally said once they were outside.

"I am," she assured him. "But I always find a way to make time for the important things."

"I'll keep that in mind," Shane responded.

Gina didn't know if he meant it or if Shane was just trying to placate her. She searched for something more to say, wanting him to stay there with her just a little bit longer.

"I appreciate you taking the time to get together with me and answering all of my questions." She knew she was repeating things, but for the moment it felt as if her brain had completely dried up. "I really did enjoy talking with you."

They were outside just beyond the coffee shop now and Shane was standing very close to her. So close that she could feel her skin warming as that old feeling that only he could create within her began to churn, taking possession of her entire being.

He was so close to her, she could feel his breath on her face—or was that wishful thinking?

Even so, for a split second, she thought Shane was going to kiss her. The very idea made her pulse begin to accelerate, causing her heart to pound. She found herself willing him to kiss her.

But then, as if breaking the spell, Shane took a step back from her. And just like that, the moment was gone.

"Yeah, well, I decided that you deserved an explanation," he said very casually. Rousing himself, Shane told her, "I guess I'll be seeing you at the shower."

Gina smiled at him widely, doing her best to sound nonchalant. "Absolutely. I'll be the woman running back and forth, doing my best to make sure everything is going smoothly," she said with a laugh.

The sun was so bright where they were standing, it was weaving golden streaks through her hair. For just an instant, Shane found himself catapulted back a decade. Feelings were attempting to work their way in.

He forced himself to block those memories. That trusting man with the loving heart was gone now.

"That sounds pretty exhausting," Shane commented on her description.

"It is," she agreed. "But it's also pretty rewarding in its own way."

Gina had almost slipped and used her usual line about helming the weddings: that there was nothing like knowing that she helped make someone's dream of a perfect wedding come true. She knew that would only remind Shane that she had torpedoed *his* dream of their wedding as well as their future together.

So she forced a cheerful smile to her lips and said, "Tell Ellie I said hi and that she's a very lucky little girl."

He knew where she was going with this and he wasn't about to let her flatter him. "I'm the lucky one," Shane contradicted. "Taking care of her gives my life purpose."

And then, like a polite stranger, he was putting his hand out to her. "Goodbye, Gina."

"Goodbye." The words all but stuck to the roof of her mouth.

She put her hand in his and shook it, thinking how painfully civilized this all seemed.

As they parted and went their separate ways, she was back to wondering if perhaps Shane still hadn't forgiven her.

Or, if he had, for some reason he hadn't done it completely.

She needed to find a way to have Shane look at her the way he used to before she'd allowed her insecurities to ruin everything. Gina desperately wanted to turn back the clock because somewhere along the line, in that brief encounter they'd just had over overpriced coffee, she realized all too clearly that she still loved him.

It wasn't just a matter of wanting something she couldn't have, thereby making it more desirable. This was a matter of bringing to attention what she had known all along in the back of her mind. That when she had fallen in love with Shane the first time, it was meant to be forever.

Maybe that was what had frightened her so badly, causing her to make the worst mistake of her life. She loved Shane so fiercely, she was afraid that he couldn't possibly love her the same way. And when he had impulsively proposed to her right after graduation, she was certain he'd regret it before the ink had time to dry on their license.

Afraid of having her heart broken, she'd turned down the proposal. But not the man. However, all he knew was that she had turned him down and that was where all their trouble started.

It was suddenly all so clear to her now, like an epiphany coming out of nowhere and dawning on her.

Now all she had to do was find a way to explain it to Shane. In order to get Shane to listen to her, she needed to get him to be open to what she had to say.

That would require finesse.

She bit her lower lip. Right now, the way to Shane's heart was through Ellie. Since she thought the little girl was adorable, this wouldn't really involve any deception on her part—just a clever approach.

Gina was smiling broadly, humming to herself by the time she got home.

Her smile lasted long enough for her to open her front door and walk in. That was when her cell phone suddenly began playing the first few bars of "Happy Days Are Here Again," letting her know that she'd just received a text message.

Hoping that Shane had had a change of heart and wanted to get together, Gina opened her phone to discover that the text wasn't from him at all.

It was from Sylvie.

Her current client had texted "9-1-1" followed by five exclamation points.

Rather than exchanging a whole slew of text messages, she thought it would just be simpler to call the bride-to-be instead.

"Hi, Sylvie, it's Gina." Anything else she was about to say was tabled when she heard the sob coming from the other end of her call.

"Oh, Gina, thank God! This is awful. You've just got to help me!" Sylvie cried.

The way Sylvie's voice was rising and falling in between sobs, Gina guessed that the woman was pacing, which only seemed to add to her agitation.

"That's what I'm here for," Gina told her cheerfully, her soothing voice cutting through the sobs. "What seems to be the problem?"

"It's not a problem, it's a total disaster!" Sylvie wailed.

Okay, Gina thought, rephrasing her question. "What is the disaster?"

Sylvie took a moment to get her voice under control before proceeding. "Well, you know I was supposed to get married in St. John's Church," the woman said, her voice still bordering on hysterical.

"Yes?" Gina encouraged.

"Well, Father Joseph said we can't use the church. Gina, it's too late to get another church. The wedding's in less than three weeks!"

Sylvie sounded as if she was on the verge of having a complete meltdown. Gina summoned her calmest voice and spoke gently to the young woman. "I know when the wedding is, Sylvie. Take a deep breath," she counseled, "and then tell me exactly what Father Joseph said to you. *Why* can't you use the church? Whatever the reason is, I'll fix it." She knew the unrealistic promise was the only way to at least partially calm the woman down.

"Because there's a huge hole in the roof!" Sylvie cried.

Well, that definitely was a reason, Gina thought. But this wasn't making any sense. Holes don't just suddenly appear.

"How did it happen, Sylvie?" Maybe the bride was exaggerating, she thought hopefully. She just needed to get to the bottom of this.

"You know that big wind that picked up after midnight last night?" Sylvie said, her voice hitching as she explained. "The big elm tree next to the church, one of its branches broke and went right through the roof. It's a disaster," she sobbed again. "Father Joseph said it wouldn't be safe to conduct the wedding in the church. He's even suspending all the masses at the church until they can come up with the funds to pay for someone to repair the roof."

Gina waited for more. When Sylvie didn't add anything, Gina said, "And that's it?" Surely there had to be an insurance policy to cover this, she thought.

"What do you mean 'and that's it?'" Sylvie cried, stunned. "That's *everything*! All my life I've dreamed of having a big church wedding and now it's not going to happen." She was sobbing again. "The wedding's off!" she declared miserably. "I can't get married!"

"Don't go canceling anything yet," Gina warned her soothingly. "Let me see what I can do."

"You fix roofs?" Sylvie questioned in disbelief.

She thought of Tiffany's husband. Eddie was a contractor. He had to be able to get someone for this job. "Not directly," Gina answered, her mind going a mile a minute. "Just hang in there. I'll get back to you in the morning."

"What am I supposed to do until morning?" Sylvie cried, back on the edge again.

"Sleep comes to mind."

"Sleep? How am I supposed to sleep when my wedding's disintegrating right in front of me?" Sylvie wailed.

She was really earning her fee this time, Gina thought. "Sylvie, getting worked up isn't going to change anything. Let me handle this."

"And you'll call me to tell me what's happening?" the overwrought bride asked nervously.

"Yes. As soon as I can get it to happen," Gina told her pointedly. "Now please, get some rest and let me do my job."

Gina paused, waiting to see if Sylvie had anything else she wanted to ask or say. For the moment, the bride-to-be's ragged breathing had subsided. She was breathing evenly and, for the moment, she was silent. Gina took that as her cue to terminate the call.

The second she ended the connection, she initiated a call to her sister. She counted the number of rings in her head, hoping she wasn't going to wind up talking to Tiffany's voicemail.

She heard Tiffany come on the line just after the fourth ring. Thank goodness!

"Tiffany, I need your help," Gina told her. "I have a four-alarm emergency on my hands."

Tiffany was perplexed when she responded. "A personal emergency or a professional bridesmaid emergency?" her sister asked.

"The latter," Gina told her.

"And just how does this professional bridesmaid emergency involve me?" Tiffany asked.

She knew she had to word this carefully. "How would your wonderful husband want to have his spot in heaven guaranteed?" Gina asked.

Tiffany sighed. "Well, to begin with, it would help if you spoke English."

Gina gave her the short version. "The church where my latest client was all set to get married has suddenly closed its doors to everyone because, thanks to that freak storm last night, they have a huge hole in their roof where the tree branch landed." She was hoping the situation was better than it sounded, but until she went out to investigate it herself, she had to rely on what Sylvie had told her.

"Well, unless that hole is the size of an abyss, I'm sure they can have it fixed," Tiffany told her.

"They probably can," Gina agreed, "but I got the impression that the congregation needs to raise the funds first and if that's the case, that's going to take time."

It dawned on Tiffany where her sister was going with this. "And you want Eddie to fix it for free," she guessed. "Gina, I can't ask him to—"

"Not for free," Gina insisted. "It's probably covered by insurance. But if there's a problem, I'm sure that Father Joseph is an honest man. Once he gets those parishioners back in their pews and starts passing around the collection plate, Eddie will start seeing the money come rolling in. In the meantime, he'll have the good feeling of knowing that he did something noble for his local church. I've seen his people do work. It takes them three days for a whole roof. This is only part of a roof. Piece of cake," she pleaded.

"I don't know, Gina…"

She could hear her sister biting her lower lip in indecision the way she did when they were kids. Gina tried to close the gap. "Did I mention it's an emergency?" she stressed.

"You did," Tiffany answered.

"I can come over right now and talk to Eddie myself about this," Gina offered. She liked her brother-in-law and for the most part, they got along well.

"Please don't," Tiffany said, vetoing the idea. She was being protective of her husband. The last thing she wanted was to be caught in the middle. "You're like a pit bull. Once you clamp your jaws down on something, you don't let go until you've worn the person down."

Gina laughed at the image. "You say that like it's a bad thing."

"All depends on what you're clamping down on," Tiffany answered wearily. "Let me talk to Eddie about this. I'll wait until he's receptive and then broach the subject with him."

"Don't wait too long," Gina cautioned. "We're fighting the clock on this one."

"What's your alternative?" Tiffany asked. "Doing it yourself?"

"I am handy," Gina pointed out.

"Right," Tiffany scoffed. "Hold on to your tool belt, Gee. There's a world of difference between banging a nail into a wall and repairing a roof. I'll call you after I talk to Eddie."

"Tell him a lot of people's happiness is at stake here," Gina added, hoping that would do the trick. Eddie was a good guy.

Tiffany laughed. "I guess Mom's not the only one who knows how to wield guilt like it's an ancient saber," she said to her sister.

"Not guilt," Gina corrected. "In this case it's just simple fact. If the roof isn't fixed, the church'll remain closed. If the church remains closed, then my bride and her groom have nowhere to get married. I gathered that neither city hall nor a backyard are alternative venues in this case. So, if they don't get married—"

"I get the picture," Tiffany said wearily, stopping her sister before she could get too carried away. "Now hang up so I can go and nag my husband into doing this."

"No, not nag. Put him in a good mood and *then* ask him to do it, remember?" Gina said, reminding her sister of what Tiffany had told her more than once.

"Since when did you get so good at playing the husband/ wife game?" Tiffany asked.

"I've been taking notes, watching you," Gina teased. "Now go and plead my case with that skillful contractor of yours before I decide to do this job myself."

Gina found herself talking to dead air. Smiling, she put her phone down. "Thanks, Tiffany," she murmured. "I owe you one."

Chapter Ten

Why was it that she had all this fortitude and the courage of her convictions when she had to sell her unusual abilities to total strangers, but when it came to approaching Shane and his niece, Gina felt her steel backbone suddenly dissolving until it had the consistency of lukewarm water?

After all, she wasn't coming to see him in order to ask Shane to do anything other than what he had already agreed to do. As a matter of fact, she thought as she slowly made her way from her parked car to the entrance of his shop on extremely rubbery legs, she wasn't asking him to do anything at all.

She was coming by to bring a peace offering of sorts. It wasn't even for him. It was for his niece, Ellie. Granted it was a thinly veiled attempt to make friends with the little girl.

Kids, especially those under ten, had always been her

weakness. Maybe because she'd longed to have kids of her own almost from the time that she was old enough to be able to have them.

Yes, she admitted, stepping up to the sidewalk, there was a small part of her that thought if she made friends with Ellie then talking with Shane would become that much easier, but that wasn't her primary focus for coming here. The little girl looked as if she needed something to play with, something to divert and hold her attention while she was here at the shop. The last time she was here, it occurred to Gina that Shane was obviously too busy to spend the kind of time with his niece that she needed.

In any case, what did she have to lose giving Ellie this gift? At the very least, Shane would just shoot her down and make her leave, although she hoped that he'd keep her offering and let Ellie have it.

Unless, of course, he was still secretly harboring a grudge.

Gina shifted the gift to the other side, putting her hand on the doorknob.

Okay, here goes nothing.

Taking a deep breath, she opened the door and walked into the airy shop.

The bell overhead tinkled, announcing her presence, although that wasn't necessary this time. Shane was out in the showroom, talking to a heavyset woman who was punctuating every word she uttered with a profusion of animated hand gestures. Gina saw him looking in her direction when the bell announced her entrance and for a second, she thought that Shane almost looked relieved to see her. And then he raised his eyebrow in an unspoken question, nodding at what she was holding.

She caught her lower lip between her teeth, wondering if that was a signal for her to come forward and say something.

And then she didn't have to.

"Why don't I give you some time to look through these photographs taken of some of the cakes I created for other weddings, Mrs. Watkins. Maybe you'll see something that will inspire you," he told the woman in an even cadence, "while I see what I can do to help this lady."

Mrs. Watkins didn't look as if she welcomed sharing his attention with someone else, but since she obviously still hadn't made up her mind, the woman grudgingly inclined her head.

"Go ahead," she murmured coldly.

"Looks like 'Cassidy' has his hands full," Gina observed with a smile, keeping her voice low as she referred to him by the name she assumed he used in the shop.

"So do you," Shane commented, nodding at the large stuffed dog she was carrying. It looked like an oversize Labrador. "New friend?"

For a second, watching Shane with the woman, she'd forgotten she was carrying this large stuffed offering. "This? It's not for me," Gina answered. "But I thought that maybe Ellie might like him." She shifted the toy to look down at its face. It was almost life-like. "I thought I could give it to her to keep her company while she's here. Unless you'd rather I didn't give it to her," she said, backtracking.

She didn't want Shane thinking she was presuming anything. She was clearly giving him the option of refusing the toy, although why he should was totally beyond her.

Shane looked the stuffed animal over and then smiled. "Thank you. That's very thoughtful of you."

She offered the Labrador to him, but he didn't take it. Instead, he walked back toward the rear door and pushed it slightly open.

"Ellie, can you come out here, please?" Shane called to his niece.

The next moment Ellie bounced into the showroom as if she had literally launched herself from a trampoline. Mrs. Watkins stopped looking through the album of photographs and appeared startled. Her round face transformed into a mask of disapproval.

"You have *children* in here?" she questioned, saying the word "children" in the same disdainful tone she would have used to say "rats."

"Not children," Shane corrected, smiling at Ellie. "Just her."

Mrs. Watkins sniffed. Gina found herself pitying any child the woman might have raised. "Isn't that disruptive in a place like this?" the woman asked, clearly showing that *she* thought it was.

"On the contrary, I find having Ellie around inspiring," Shane said, addressing his words affectionately to his niece.

Ellie shifted so that she could look up at her uncle and beamed.

"Oh," Mrs. Watkins huffed, and then she visibly retreated.

Ellie, meanwhile, was oblivious to the exchange going on around her. Her eyes were almost saucer wide as she stared at the stuffed dog that Gina was holding. The little girl who had literally bounced into the room now took a tentative step toward the stuffed animal.

"Can I touch it?" she asked Gina almost shyly.

"You can do anything you want with it," Gina told Ellie with a broad smile. "It's yours."

Ellie's mouth dropped open. "Mine?" she asked in almost a hushed voice. The next second, her head swiveled toward her uncle. "Really?" she squealed.

"That's between you and Miss Bongino, peanut," Shane told his niece.

"Miss Bon-Bongee—" Ellie was obviously having trouble saying Gina's name.

Gina tried not to laugh. She didn't want to hurt the girl's feelings. "Just say 'Gina,' Ellie. It's much easier," Gina told her.

Ellie looked at her uncle. "Is that okay?" she asked.

"That's up to Miss Gina," he said, sticking in just a small sign of respect for the girl to use. "If it's okay with her, it's okay with me," Shane told her.

It was easy to see by the look on his face that although Shane was trying to raise the little girl with some rules, he completely doted on her.

"Well, now that we've got *that* out of the way," Gina said to the little girl, "I think that it's time that you and Robby got acquainted."

"Is that his name?" Ellie asked, still looking at the stuffed animal as if she expected him to take off at any second.

"Unless you'd like to change it," Gina said, offering Ellie the option to do just that.

Ellie looked as if she thought that was sacrilege. "Uh-uh," she answered, emphatically vetoing any kind of a name change. "He might not like that."

"I see," Gina said, trying hard not to laugh.

Accepting the incredibly soft stuffed dog into her

arms, Ellie looked slightly overwhelmed by it. The little girl buried her face in the dog's side.

"It's so soft," she marveled. And then she looked up at Gina. "I can really keep him?" she asked in awed disbelief.

Gina nodded, offering an encouraging smile. "Absolutely."

Ellie squealed, burying her face against the stuffed dog again. And then, without any warning, she propped up the dog against the counter on the floor—it was almost the size of an actual small Labrador—and threw her arms around Gina, giving her a really fierce hug.

Gina was surprised at the amount of strength the little girl exhibited.

"Thank you!" Ellie cried.

How those simple words affected her. Gina thought her heart would burst. "My pleasure, baby. My pleasure," she assured the little girl, stroking her blond head.

The other woman in the showroom cleared her throat rather loudly. When Shane looked in her direction, she coldly announced, "If you're through humoring the child, I'm ready to tell you what I want for my daughter's wedding cake."

Shane was quiet for a moment, as if debating what he was about to say. And then he decided to say it. "You know what, Mrs. Watkins? I just rechecked my schedule again when I ducked into the back and I'm not going to be able to create that cake for your daughter's wedding after all." Mrs. Watkins's face fell, but he went on talking as if he hadn't noticed. "I'm just too booked up."

"But you have to," Mrs. Watkins insisted, completely appalled.

"No, I don't," Shane countered, his voice firm, his position steadfast.

The gray-haired woman was utterly stunned. Momentarily at a loss for words, she finally cried, "Well, what am I supposed to do now?" Her tone was totally accusatory.

"I'm afraid I haven't the vaguest idea," Shane replied, beginning to guide her toward his door. "But I am sure that a resourceful woman such as yourself will be able to figure it out."

Mrs. Watkins sputtered several times, although nothing intelligible sounding came out of her mouth. Finally, seeing that "Cassidy" was not about to change his mind, she stormed out, slamming the door so hard in her wake that it reverberated throughout the small, tidy shop.

Gina watched the door, holding her breath. Afraid that Mrs. Watkins would come stomping back in. Or, at the very least, that the glass in the upper portion of the door would shatter.

But the glass remained intact as the noise slowly abated. And then another, less threatening sound replaced the sound of the slamming door. It was the sound of Gina clapping her hands.

Ellie looked up at her new friend quizzically. "Why are you clapping?" she asked. "There's nobody singing or dancing like the shows I get to watch on my TV."

"I'm clapping because your uncle did something very brave," Gina explained to the little girl.

Ellie's small face was a mask of surprise and wonder as she looked from Gina to her uncle and then back again. It was clear that she didn't understand and she wanted to.

"He did?" she questioned.

Gina's eyes met Shane's. And then her lips curved as she nodded.

"Yup, he did. Can you afford to turn business away?" she asked him, worried about what the noble move might have cost him.

"I can if it means working for someone like that. I have to at least like the person I'm creating the cake for," Shane told her. "I have a feeling that Mrs. Watkins wasn't going to allow her daughter to have a say in any of this. The woman is a dictator with a mean streak a mile wide. It was obvious that she wants to be involved in the process from start to finish." He shook his head. "I can't work like that."

Ellie seemed oblivious to her uncle's explanation. Instead, she had a question for him out of the blue. "Do you like Gina?"

Shane looked down at his niece, stunned. Where had that come from? He knew he hadn't said anything to make Ellie think that he had any sort of feelings about Gina one way or another. Maybe he'd misunderstood her.

"What?"

"Do you like Gina?" Ellie repeated. "'Cause I like her," she told him matter-of-factly, wrapping her arms more tightly around the stuffed dog.

Now he understood. "That's because she just bought you off with that mutt," Shane said with a laugh.

"I wasn't trying to buy her off," Gina protested. "I thought that if Ellie had something fun to play with, you could get more work done," she explained.

"So you did have an ulterior motive," Shane concluded.

Gina didn't know if he was just kidding or being serious. She certainly couldn't tell by his expression.

She decided to sidestep his insinuation altogether and only said, "I'm just trying to be helpful." Feeling that it was safer, she shifted her focus to Ellie. "You know when I was your age, Ellie, I had a stuffed tiger I took everywhere."

Ellie looked up, interested. "What was his name?" she asked.

"His name was Timmy," Gina told her.

She answered his niece's question so easily, Shane thought that maybe Gina had actually had a stuffed tiger by that name.

"Where's Timmy now?" Ellie asked, then added hopefully, "Maybe he and Robby can play."

Gina flashed the little girl a sad smile. "I'm afraid I don't have him anymore."

Ellie's face drooped in disappointment. "Where is he?"

"Timmy went to stay with some kids in a hospital oh, about twenty years ago," Gina answered. She saw the little girl's confusion and added, "Timmy liked cheering kids up and we both thought he'd be happier there where he could play with kids."

"But what about you?" Ellie asked.

Gina smiled fondly at the little girl. "I wasn't a kid anymore."

She could feel Shane looking at her but for the life of her, she couldn't begin to guess what he was thinking. Did he think that she was somewhat demented, talking about a stuffed animal as if it was real with actual feelings and the ability to think? There was a time when she *had* felt that way about some of her toys, but that had been a very long time ago.

Gina smiled, unable to help herself. That had always

been her gift. Her ability to remember what she had been like as a little girl. It helped her easily relate to children like Ellie.

Of course, that same "gift" probably made other adults think that she was slightly crazy or at least a little strange.

"What do you say to Miss Bongi—to Miss Gina?" Shane corrected himself as he prompted his niece.

If possible, Ellie's arms tightened even harder around the stuffed dog she was holding.

"Thank you, Miss Gina," Ellie declared, a smile all but vibrating in her voice. She was beaming at her as she held on to the stuffed dog.

Just hearing the little girl sound so happy was more than payment enough as far as Gina was concerned. She ran her hand over the small blond head.

"You're very welcome, Ellie," Gina told her with feeling.

Gina straightened slightly. It was time to leave. She couldn't very well just hang around here like an extra appendage, even though, secretly, she was more than willing to stay.

But she had done what she had come to do: she'd made friends with Ellie and that, in turn, had gotten Shane to see her in a better light. With a little bit of luck, she could build on that and maybe, eventually, she could work her way back to how things had once been between them. Or, at the very least, to the point where he felt less hostile to her than he had felt before this wedding had miraculously come up.

"All right then," Gina said to the little girl. "I'm glad you and Robby have hit it off so well." She turned toward

Shane who was still silently watching her. "And I'll come by on Saturday to pick up the pastries for the shower."

"There's no need for you to come by on Saturday, Gina," Shane told her in a subdued voice that set off all sorts of alarms in her head.

Oh Lord, had he changed his mind again? He couldn't do that. She'd already told Sylvie he was handling the desserts.

She needed to find a way to get him to change his mind back.

"You're not going to make the pastries after all?" Gina questioned, making no effort to hide her disappointment.

"I didn't say that," Shane pointed out quietly after a beat.

Okay, maybe she was getting ahead of herself. Gina forced herself to calm down before she asked, "All right, what *are* you saying?"

"That you don't have to come by to pick them up because I'll be delivering the pastries to the shower myself," he told her.

Yes, Virginia, she thought as relief and happiness suddenly flooded all through her insides, *there is a Santa Claus!*

Gina felt the corners of her eyes growing damp. The man just kept on surprising her.

Chapter Eleven

There were no new panicky calls from Sylvie—for which Gina was extremely grateful because that meant she had no new fires to put out. Knowing this could change at any moment, Gina decided to go see her brother-in-law and find out firsthand if Eddie was going to be able to fit in making the necessary repairs on the church's roof in time for the wedding.

Thinking she needed better information herself, she drove by the church first. She wanted to get an idea of how bad the damage actually was.

It was bad.

That was the first thought that hit her as Gina drove into the church's near-empty parking lot.

She could see the damage even before she came to a full stop. More than fifty years ago, someone, presumably a well-meaning parishioner, had planted a California pepper tree next to the church. Pictures of the area indicated that it had been little more than a sapling when it had been planted. But it had long since become an accident waiting to happen.

And then it did.

Getting out of her car, Gina slowly walked around the church and surveyed the damage. It was lucky that it had happened at night and not during the daytime, or on a Sunday when there might have been a lot of people attending a service.

Someone really could have gotten hurt then. At least this way, the only thing that had suffered was the roof and part of the inside of the church.

"Could have been worse."

Caught off guard, Gina didn't jump when she heard the deep voice coming from behind her. She'd recognize her brother-in-law's rumbling cadence anywhere.

Turning around to face him, she smiled up at the tall, lanky man with his permanently unruly chestnut hair.

"Hi, Eddie. Thanks for coming out. Can you fix it?" she asked him hopefully.

Her brother-in-law had his clipboard in his hands and was writing things down even as he talked to her. "Of course I can fix it," he answered. "The problem is, do I have the time?"

"If you need an extra body, I can help," she quickly offered.

He laughed dryly. "That'll take me twice as long, then."

Gina pretended to be offended, although she knew he was teasing her. She also knew that he was better off using trained workers than taking her up on her offer. "I'm not that bad," she protested.

Eddie looked up from the clipboard and rolled his eyes. "All I need is you falling off the roof and I'll have my wife and your mother on my case for the rest of my natural life. Maybe longer. No thank you, Gee."

Gina nodded. "All right, what *can* I do to help?"

He went back to working on his notes. "Just let me make my assessment of the damage and what it'll take to fix it. Then you can go and make arrangements with the local padre—"

"Monsignor," Gina corrected.

Eddie waved his hand. "Whatever. The head guy," he said, using the all-purpose term, "to give my company the authorization to get the job done."

She knew she should just back off and leave him to his estimate, but she was anxious. "When do you think you can finish it?" Gina asked.

Eddie never looked up. "In a month," he answered.

"Eddie!" Gina cried, distressed.

He raised his head, briefly focusing on his sister-in-law. "The job'll take four days. Finding the time to do it in, however, is going to be trickier," he told her honestly.

Gina moved around so that she was able to get into his face. She gave him her most soulful expression. "I'm counting on you, Eddie."

"Great. Pressure. Just what I need as an incentive," Tiffany's husband murmured under his breath. And then he said more audibly, "All I can say is that I'll do my best."

That was as good as a promise, Gina thought. "Knew I could count on you," she cried, giving Eddie a quick, grateful kiss on the cheek. "Tell Tiffany I said she married a great guy."

He laughed dryly. "I tell her that all the time. She doesn't seem to be convinced," Eddie told her, walking away.

Tuning his sister-in-law out, Eddie continued making notations to himself about the job.

Gina left him to it and slipped away quietly.

"It's all under control," Gina informed Sylvie for the third time in as many days.

It was the day of the bridal shower and the nervous bride had confronted her in person the moment she had walked into Sylvie's sister's house. Sylvie's sister, Monica, was her maid of honor and the Jack and Jill bridal shower was being held in her house.

"You're sure?" Sylvie asked, and her voice went up so high, it was almost a squeak. Gina winced as the piercing sound penetrated her ears. It was going to undoubtedly haunt her dreams for a good while to come, if not forever.

"Very sure," Gina assured her as serenely as possible. "I was there yesterday and I spoke to Father Joseph who, in turn, had spoken to Monsignor McGuire about the whole thing." She smiled broadly. "The upshot is that they gave the go-ahead for the work to commence and the church will be ready in time for your wedding. My brother-in-law's company is handling the repairs and you couldn't be in better hands," Gina guaranteed.

"Relax, Sylvie," she calmly instructed the bride. "If you keep this up, you're going to worry yourself into a hospital bed before the wedding ever takes place."

"You're right," Sylvie agreed, blowing out a long

breath. "You're absolutely right." She flashed a spasmodic smile that vanished as quickly as it had appeared. "It's just that—"

"It's just that nothing," Gina informed her, putting an end to any further protest from the bride-to-be. "In the blink of an eye, this will all be over and you will have missed it because you wound up worrying yourself to a frazzle," she told her client. "This is your wedding shower, Sylvie. Enjoy it."

Gina saw Sylvie's face suddenly brightening.

"There, that's better," she congratulated her client— and then she realized that the woman was looking at something over her shoulder.

Turning around Gina could see Shane walking in through the front door. He was carrying a very large box embossed with his logo on it: Cakes Created by Cassidy.

"If you'll excuse me," Gina said, stepping away from Sylvie. "I think the pastries for your shower have arrived."

Weaving around the several guests who had arrived early and were in the process of mingling, Gina made her way over toward Shane.

"Hi! You made it," Gina declared, smiling up at his handsome, chiseled blond features and beautiful blue eyes.

Shane turned toward her. He wasn't surprised to see Gina there ahead of him. "Didn't you think I would?" he questioned.

"Of course I did," she answered, scrambling to correct any misimpression she might have created. She didn't want him thinking that she didn't have any faith in his word. "It's just that, well, things happen in my line of work. Sometimes the best laid plans, etcetera, etcetera…" Gina said, allowing her voice to trail off. Changing the subject, she said, "That smells wonderful." Gina nodded at the box.

In all honesty, she meant that *he* smelled wonderful, although she knew that she couldn't say that. She'd caught a faint whiff of cologne when someone opened the door just now. Unless she had totally lost her mind, Shane had on the same cologne he used to wear when they were going together. The scent always made her feel nostalgic.

Every so often, whenever she caught a hint of the cologne while passing someone in a restaurant or in a store, old memories would come flooding back to her. Memories accompanied by that longing she always experienced whenever she thought of Shane and all the things that might have been.

If only…

"Where do you want this?" Shane asked, nodding at the box he was holding.

"I just got here myself," she told him, looking around. "But my guess would be over there." Gina pointed to a table that was set up against one of the family room walls.

The next moment, the question of where to put the pastries was solved.

"Hi, I'm Monica," a tall, statuesque brunette said, introducing herself as she came over to join them, or rather Shane, Gina thought. "I'm Sylvie's maid of honor in charge of this little shindig and yes, that's where all the food is going." Putting one hand on Shane's wrist to hold him in place, Monica used her other hand to lift the lid on the box he had brought in. "That looks really tempting," she told him with an appreciative sigh.

Something told Gina that from the way Monica was looking at Shane, she wasn't really talking about the pastries.

This was no time to give in to jealousy, Gina silently upbraided herself. She was here in a professional capacity, despite the pretty invitation that had arrived in the mail. Besides, she didn't own Shane. He was certainly free to pay attention and receive attention from anyone he chose.

"There're more boxes of pastries in the car," Shane replied.

"Oh, I can help you bring them in," Monica quickly volunteered.

If her smile were any wider, Gina thought, Shane was in serious danger of falling in.

Shane didn't seem to take note of the fact that the woman's eyes were gleaming at him.

"That's all right," he told Sylvie's maid of honor. "Gina already volunteered to help me with them. Gina?" he asked as he turned toward the doorway and began heading back outside again.

"I'm right here," Gina assured him, picking up her pace in order to keep up with Shane.

The man had eight inches on her and it was all leg, she thought, hurrying.

"I hope you don't mind helping out," Shane said to her as soon as they had cleared the house. "It's just that I think the bride's maid of honor had more than just pastries on her mind and I don't like things getting complicated."

Gina struggled not to laugh. Instead, she said playfully, "Always happy to help you beat them off with a stick."

Shane cleared his throat, although he didn't appear embarrassed. "I didn't mean to sound conceited."

"You didn't," she quickly assured him. "You can't help it if women are attracted to your tall, blond good looks." She wasn't teasing him. She meant what she was saying.

Shane's laugh was self-deprecating. He shook his head. "I guess I deserve that."

"No," Gina told him. *But I do. I deserve you,* she thought. *I just have to get you to realize that.*

There were four more boxes filled with the pastries he'd made for this occasion. They were carefully arranged in the back of his SUV.

Gina looked in. "You certainly brought a lot."

"In my experience," he told her, "people tend to get very hungry at these things. Better to bring more than not enough."

She lifted out a box, then waited for him to do the same. "You are staying for this, aren't you?" Gina asked him. She had learned that taking anything for granted was always a mistake.

There was a slight frown on his face which told her that Shane was far from happy about the demands this situation placed on him.

"Only until it's politely acceptable for me to make my exit," he told her. About to reach in to take a box, he paused and looked at her, searching her face. "Why?"

She didn't try to sound clever. Honesty was her best policy when it came to Shane. "Because I have to stay," she told Shane, "and it would be nice if I had a friend to talk to."

He surprised her by laughing. "As I recall, you never had any trouble when it came to talking."

"I said *a friend* to talk to," Gina pointed out, repeating what she'd said.

Rather than taking Gina up on her offer, he pointed out, "You don't have to stay."

"Oh, but I'm afraid that I do," Gina contradicted. "My job is to make sure that no emergencies—big or small—arise from the moment the bride hires me until she and the groom have their last dance and make their escape to begin either their honeymoon or start their blissful life together."

"Blissful, eh?" Shane repeated. Was it her imagination, or did he look amused? "Is that part of your guarantee, too?"

"No, that part is up to them," Gina told him seriously. "I just try to make sure that everything leading up to that point paves the way for that to happen for them. If it doesn't…" She lifted her shoulders in a careless shrug. "Well, at least I know that I tried my best."

For the first time since she ran into him, Shane's mouth curved in a lopsided grin. She'd forgotten until this moment how much she used to love seeing that.

"As I recall," he told her, "your best was more than good enough."

It was a moment of weakness and Shane knew it. But he couldn't seem to help himself. As they stood next to his SUV right over the two boxes of pastries they were about to carry into the house, Shane leaned over and kissed her. The second he did, he was instantly propelled back through time and space, back to when there had been no hurt feelings, no rejections, no oceans separating them and all the things that might have been.

The second his lips touched hers, Gina felt as if her heart was going to explode right then and there.

She had *never* thought she would feel like this again, never thought she could be this happy again. And yet, here she was, being swept away the way she always was whenever he had kissed her.

Her heart went into double time. She could barely catch her breath.

And then, just as quickly as it had happened, it was over.

Shane drew back, the look on his face all but telling her that he felt he had made a mistake. When he spoke, he just compounded the jagged, painful sensations she was feeling.

"Sorry," he told her. "I didn't mean to do that. I guess, just for a second, I forgot who we were." The words were stilted. Awkward. "It won't happen again."

Her eyes searched Shane's face, looking for a trace of the man who had once loved her. The man who she still loved.

He wasn't there.

"Even if I want it to?" Gina asked, addressing the words to his retreating back.

Shane stopped walking for a moment. She thought he was going to turn around and say something to her, maybe even answer her question.

But he just continued walking as if he hadn't heard her. Or worse, didn't think that she deserved an answer.

Taking a breath, she willed her feet to move and followed Shane into the house.

"Here, let me help you," Monica said, suddenly meeting them in the doorway. "These must be heavy." She raised her eyes to his face. "It took you a while to carry them in."

Her words were for Shane, not her, Gina realized.

The maid of honor took the box from Shane. "You can get the rest—if there's more," she added with what Gina was certain the woman thought appeared to be an attractive pout.

"There's more," Shane answered.

"Wonderful!" Monica gushed. "I'll tell Allison to make room on the buffet table." The woman strode quickly with the big box. Putting it down, she looked ready to escort Shane back out to his SUV.

Gina was tempted to put the box she'd brought in down on the first flat surface so she could go back out and rescue Shane, but then she rethought the matter.

Maybe he didn't want to be rescued, she told herself. Maybe Shane preferred someone who he had no history with. Someone with a clean slate, at least where he was concerned.

In any event, she silently told herself, Shane was a big boy and could more than take care of himself. After all, he had just proved it with her.

Chapter Twelve

For the next few hours, Gina remained at the bridal shower, keeping to the background as she watched to make sure that everything at the party went off without a hitch. She felt that it was her job to make sure that everyone had a good time.

She managed to do it all while staying close to Shane. What made it even better was that he remained with her by his own choice, not hers.

Because of that, Sylvie's maid of honor threw her a number of dirty looks, but Gina fended them all off with a smile. She acted completely impervious to them as well as to the scowl on Monica's face as the latter shot daggers in her direction.

"I have a feeling that when I leave this party, the maid of honor is going to try to run me over with her car," she confided to Shane in a low voice. When he looked at her, his eyebrows raised in a silent query, Gina found herself laughing. "I'm just kidding, although I'm pretty sure I won't be making Monica's Christmas card list this year."

Sitting off to the side, out of the way, Shane took in what was going on around him. He could remember a time when parties were a prominent part of his week ends, but now he preferred to spend his time more quietly.

He was well aware of the way that the maid of honor was looking at him. Like she was a hungry cat and he was the last morsel of food left in the area.

Inclining his head toward Gina, he said quietly, "Thanks for doing this."

She knew he meant, in essence, having her behave like a roadblock for him. "Hey, I'm the reason you're here to begin with, so I kind of owe this to you," she said, shrugging off his thanks.

"Well, you can get back to mingling in a few minutes," he told her. "It looks like no one has any complaints about the pastries, so I'm going to be leaving soon."

"So soon?" Gina asked, not bothering to hide her regret.

"Soon?" Shane repeated, glancing at his watch. "I've been here over two hours."

"*Almost* two hours. That's really not very much time. You could stay a little longer," she coaxed, trying her best to sound casual.

"Maybe I would under normal circumstances," he allowed, "but Ellie was coming down with a cold when I left today and I like being around when she's not feeling well."

He had really become a homebody. Who would have guessed? "Does she have a temperature?" she asked him.

"It had gone down when I left, but you know kids." The inference in his voice was that he assumed she knew all about the fevers they could run at times.

"Only by reputation," Gina quipped. "And, of course, there is my niece. You know," she recalled fondly, "when I was a kid, any time I was sick, my mother made me chicken soup—from scratch, not out of a can. And she always gave me comic books to read. It got to the point that I used to look forward to being sick." Gina grinned at him. "One time I tried to fool my mother by holding a thermometer over an open flame on the stove. It registered really high and I got busted—when the thermometer did."

Shane's laugh blended with hers. Gina felt a warm shiver washing over her.

"Can't fool mothers," he murmured as if it was a private joke that just the two of them shared. Taking a breath, Shane set the glass of punch he'd been nursing for the better part of the last two hours on the table. "I'd better get going." He hesitated for a moment, then said, "Give me a call in case someone finds the pastries not to their liking."

All Gina heard was that he was asking her to call him. It wasn't easy to keep from grinning from ear to ear. "So you're really serious about taking in complaints?"

"I'm open to constructive criticism," Shane told her.

For a second, she debated keeping quiet. He might just think she was trying to flatter him. But not saying anything just wasn't her way, so she asked, "Want my opinion?"

He looked at her, not sure what to expect. "Go ahead."

"You know you're really good at what you do," Gina told him. She'd sampled a few of his creations and each one was better than the last. "Those pastries are out of this world. You don't need to hear some person who's trying to build up their own ego by coming down hard on what is clearly a wonderful effort. The only way those pastries you 'created' could taste better is if they were served in heaven."

Shane laughed at that, really laughed. And just as he took his leave, she noticed that the wariness she'd detected earlier was gone from his eyes. The walls between them were finally breaking down, Gina thought with relief. There really was hope!

Though it wasn't easy, she curbed her desire to walk with Shane to the front door. She didn't want him to feel that she was crowding him.

Just as she was holding herself in check, Gina saw Monica come hurrying over to Shane as he reached the front door. The maid of honor looked as if she was attempting to draw Shane aside under some pretext, but she saw him shaking his head and then leaving within a couple of minutes despite all of Monica's efforts to the contrary.

Gina's triumphant feeling faded as she glanced at her watch. She couldn't leave yet. There were at least two more hours of this to go.

Putting a smile on her face, Gina made the best of it.

It wasn't easy, but she refrained from calling Shane when she finally left the bridal shower some three hours later. Fighting the impulse to fly out of there, she adhered to her obligations. That meant remaining at the bridal shower until the last of the guests had trickled away.

On the plus side, she knew her client was extremely happy. In addition, keeping her ears open, she was also able to collect a large number of flattering comments about the pastries that Shane had created and brought to the party.

No one, it seemed, had a single negative thing to say about them—unless she counted the fact that a couple of bridesmaids lamented that the pastries were "sinfully delicious" and impossible to stop eating. Gina had a feeling that there would be several bridesmaids whose dresses would be severely stretched to the limit.

She resisted the urge to call Shane with her "report." She even thought about skipping the call altogether and just driving up to his house to tell him in person.

Giving in to her curiosity, she had done a little research on him and apparently Shane was living in the house where he had grown up. She had always assumed that it had been sold years ago, but apparently he had hung on to it, maybe as a way of keeping the memory of his parents and brother alive. He had mentioned that there was a trust.

Gina had gone so far as to pick up her keys and head toward her car, but she talked herself out of it. Because going there now would be seen as stalking.

No, she could call him tomorrow to tell him what she'd heard people saying about his pastries. Calling him tomorrow would seem far less desperate than calling today—or showing up on his doorstep.

She knew she was doing the right thing, waiting like this. But being right wasn't nearly as much of a comfort as it should have been, Gina thought with a sigh that went clear down to her toes.

Being there with Shane in that party setting proved

to her just how much she'd really missed him all these years.

Just then, the phone in the kitchen rang, startling her. The landline sounded so much more demanding and business-like than the cell phone she kept in her pocket did.

Hurrying over to the landline, she picked up the receiver and put it against her ear. "Hello?"

"Is it over?"

It was Shane.

She basked in the sound of his voice for a second before answering. He had to realize it was over because she was here to answer the phone, but she didn't bother pointing that out.

"Yes. It ended half an hour ago. I just walked into the house this minute," she told him. Glancing around, she spotted a chair, pulled it over and sat down.

"Half an hour," he repeated as the words sank in. "And you didn't call because there were complaints," he guessed, obviously assuming the worst from her silence.

"No, I didn't call because I didn't want you to think I was stalking you," she told him honestly. "I was going to call you tomorrow—to tell you that everyone in the wedding party is cursing you."

"Cursing me? Why?" he cried, surprised.

"Because if they don't fit into their bridesmaid dresses in two weeks, it's all your fault," she told him. "You made pastries that they, no matter how good their intentions were, couldn't resist." There was silence on his end. Was he worried that she was saving the worst for last? She was quick to relieve his concerns. "There wasn't so much as a crumb left and believe me, several of the bridesmaids, not to mention the mother of the bride, checked. They even asked me if I was hiding more somewhere. Some of them saw me coming in with you, carrying one of the pastry boxes," she explained. "I'm lucky that I managed to get away from there without being tortured."

"Tortured?" Shane questioned, puzzled.

"In case I *was* hiding more pastries somewhere," she answered.

That same wonderful laugh she loved echoed against her ear, all but engulfing her. "I forgot how much you liked to exaggerate," he said.

"I'm not exaggerating this time. I think you don't realize just how good those creations of yours really are," she told him. Because she knew that Shane had always had a hard time with compliments, she changed the subject. "How's Ellie doing? Did her fever go away?" she asked him.

"That all depends on what time you're asking about," Shane told her. "When I came home, it was almost back to normal. Then an hour later, it started to climb up again. I've had three different readings since I got back. If it's like this tomorrow, I might have to take her to the walk-in clinic. Or the ER," he said, thinking that the acclaimed hospital right in the area might be his best bet.

While Gina loved the fact that he was concerned about the child, she didn't want Shane worrying to the point that he was all but wrapping the little girl in cotton.

"When they're harboring a cold, kids under the age of seven tend to run high fevers at certain times of the day, especially in the evening. It can be high when they wake up, drop to normal around noon and then go up again by six."

"You have kids?" he questioned, surprised. Shane

thought she'd said that she didn't, but maybe he'd mis-understood. Maybe there was even more about Gina that he didn't know.

"No, but I have a niece and I was there when my sister went through this." Maybe she was butting in where she wasn't wanted. This was all very new territory to her. All she could do was tell Shane the truth. "I just wanted you to know this isn't all that unusual."

"Thanks," he told her and he sounded as if he meant it. "I appreciate the pep talk."

"Anytime," Gina replied. She didn't hear a childish voice calling in the background. "Sounds quiet."

"It is," Shane agreed. "I gave Ellie some baby aspirin and she fell asleep about fifteen minutes ago."

"I'd better let you go, then," she said although she was reluctant to end the call. They were really getting along rather well at the moment. She was afraid that the second she hung up, things would revert back to what they had been just a little while ago, but that would be selfish of her. "It's important to get your rest when you can."

"That makes sense," Shane agreed. And then she heard him say, "Gina?"

About to say goodbye she stopped and held on to the phone with both hands. "Yes?"

"Thanks for calling."

Gina hesitated, torn. She didn't want to spoil the mo-ment and correct him, but if he remembered this later, he'd know that he'd gotten this wrong. She hadn't called him, he had called her. She needed to say something now before it got too awkward.

"Um, Shane?"

"Yes?"

"You were the one who called me," Gina told him.

There was silence on the other end. And then he said, "You're right. I totally forgot. Maybe I *should* get some rest."

Gina felt her smile widening. He didn't take offense at having her correct him. She took that to be a good sign.

"Good idea," she told Shane. "I'll talk to you later."

It was only after she hung up that she realized she'd all but told him that she was going to be calling back. And he hadn't objected.

So, this was what progress felt like, Gina thought, pleased.

For the first time since she had walked into the bakery and had her world blown apart when she saw Shane standing there, Gina spent a restful night.

She woke up early because that was a habit she'd developed from the time she was in grade school. Back then it was because life was an exciting adventure to her and she was afraid of missing anything, even a moment of it. She grew up, but she never outgrew that feeling.

Taking a quick shower, she made herself a slice of toast and then got down to work.

She checked her refrigerator to see what she needed to get at the store—and found that she didn't need to get anything. Her shelves were full.

"You have *got* to get another hobby besides me, Mom," she murmured. But for once, she wasn't upset about her mother dropping by with groceries. It saved her time. She found that she had all the ingredients she needed—carrots, celery and a whole chicken.

She was going to make old-fashioned chicken soup just the way her grandmother had taught her. It wasn't going to be anything elaborate, just basic ingredients, mixed in an oversize pot with water, salt and love.

Smiling, Gina got to work.

Dutifully, she turned up the flame on her stove, brought everything she'd put into the pot to a boil, then turned the flame down again until it was on medium. She partially covered the pot, then sat down in the kitchen to keep vigil for the next hour and a half. She knew the old adage about a watched pot never boiling, but she was also aware of the practical fact that unattended pots sometimes had a way of boiling over and then having their contents boil away.

Finding the timer she had stashed in a drawer, she set it for ninety minutes, then forced herself to be patient.

It was much easier said than done.

While the ingredients she had thrown together were busy becoming soup, Gina searched for something to carry it in once it was finally finished cooking and had cooled down enough to transport.

Finding something appropriate to use took her more time than putting the soup together had. But she finally found a clear airtight container she could use to bring the soup to Shane.

If Ellie was all better—and kids really did bounce back with amazing resilience—then Shane and the little girl could have the soup for lunch anyway. And if Ellie was still sick, then if the little girl was anything like she'd once been, Gina was confident that the soup would be incredibly welcome.

Gina dug a box of egg noodles out of her pantry and prepared them to go with the soup. The noodles were ready a lot sooner than the soup was. Straining the noodles, she packed them up in a separate container and went back to waiting.

Once the soup was ready and was placed, along with shredded bits of chicken, into its own container, there was only one thing missing from this meal.

But for that, Gina knew she needed to stop at a bookstore.

She glanced at her watch. Today was Sunday. The bookstores in her area didn't open until ten thirty.

Perfect timing, she thought as she moved around and got ready. Everything would be packed up and ready to go by ten thirty.

Chapter Thirteen

"But I'm all better, Unca Shane," Ellie protested, her lower lip protruding in a pout as she looked up at her uncle.

In an effort to strike an acceptable compromise with Ellie, Shane had told his niece she didn't have to stay in her bed as long as she remained on the sofa he'd made up for her in the family room. He'd placed three multicolored pillows at her back, propping her up into practically a sitting position. Shane had also tucked Ellie's favorite princess blanket all around her small body.

To keep his niece occupied, there was a collection of popular cartoons playing on the TV courtesy of the Blu-ray disk he had inserted earlier.

"Humor me, sweetie," Shane requested, ruffling her soft, silky hair. "You weren't all better last night," he reminded her.

"But that was then. This is now," Ellie insisted with the budding logic of a little woman. "I wanna play, Unca Shane."

"You can get up and play tomorrow," Shane told her. He finished his sentence quickly because he could see that Ellie was already starting to throw off her princess blanket. She gave all the signs of being ready to hop off the sofa at the slightest provocation.

"But tomorrow's school," she complained as he tucked the blanket back around her.

The sharpness of Ellie's mind never failed to amaze him. Half the time Shane felt he had trouble keeping track of what day it was, yet this little munchkin whose care he'd found himself entrusted with always seemed to be on top of everything.

"Preschool," he corrected, although he knew that to Ellie it was one and the same. "Tell you what. You stay on the sofa today like a good girl and you can stay home from preschool tomorrow."

Shane knew he had to make arrangements with Barbara, the nanny he usually had watching his niece when he worked, but that was really the easy part. Getting Ellie to stay put today was definitely going to be the difficult part. Luckily, since it was Sunday, the bakery was closed and he could stay with Ellie.

"So do we have a deal?" he asked his niece in all seriousness.

Ellie puckered up her mouth as if she was thinking over his proposition. And then she nodded, announcing with a resigned smile, "Okay, deal." Having made her declaration, she put out her hand to her uncle, wanting to shake on it.

Caught off guard, Shane realized that Ellie felt it was

part of the agreement because she had witnessed him shaking hands with one of his suppliers after a delivery had been made. He knew that reinforcement had become very important to the little girl. She needed it to make her feel secure.

Smiling at Ellie, Shane shook her hand. Just as he did, the doorbell rang. Surprised, he glanced over toward the front door.

"You expecting someone, Ellie?" Shane asked his niece, doing his best to keep a straight face.

Ellie appeared to seriously think about his question, then shook her head, her blond hair swinging about her face. "No."

"Stay there," he instructed when he saw that, prompted by her boundless curiosity, Ellie was starting to get off the sofa again.

He heard Ellie sigh mightily as he walked to the door, as if he were trying the last of her patience.

She was going to be a handful when she got older, he thought.

Preoccupied, Shane didn't look through the peephole when he reached the front door. Instead, he just opened it, and then stared in absolute surprise at the woman on his doorstep. His surprise doubled when he saw that she was holding what looked like a picnic basket and using both hands.

"Can I come in?" Gina asked when he didn't say anything. "This is getting heavy."

Coming to, Shane reached for the basket. "Here, let me take that." The first thing that hit him was that Gina wasn't exaggerating. The basket really *was* heavy. Stepping to the side, he let her in, then turned to follow her.

"Did I forget we were supposed to meet today?" he asked Gina, confused.

"No, you didn't forget anything," she replied, hoping that she hadn't made a mistake and overstepped some invisible boundary line Shane had drawn. They were making progress and she didn't want to take a chance on ruining that. But at the same time, she did want to go with her instincts. "I just thought, since you said that Ellie was sick, that I'd bring her—and you—some chicken soup. Homemade," Gina added quickly. She didn't want Shane to think she had just opened up a few cans of soup, warmed them up and then dumped them into a container. "That always made me feel better when I was Ellie's age and got sick."

He looked down at the basket he was carrying. The scent of hot chicken soup was beginning to waft up to him through everything.

"You mentioned that," he recalled. "You also said something about a comic book."

Smiling, now that her hands were free, she pulled out several comic books she'd stopped to pick up at a nearby bookstore. She had painstakingly pored over them to find just the right, age-appropriate ones to give Shane's niece.

"She doesn't already have these, does she?" she asked him.

"She doesn't have any," Shane told her.

"No comic books?" Gina asked, surprised. But then, she supposed that things like that were probably no longer in vogue for the short set. She could remember spending hours reading all sorts of comic books as a kid, everything from the adventures of a park bear and his faithful sidekick, to the ongoing crusades of an entire slew of superheroes. "Well then, she's in for a treat," Gina promised him.

"Who's there, Unca Shane?" Ellie called out, craning her neck and getting up as far as she could on the sofa without actually coming off it. She knew her uncle wouldn't be happy if she did.

"Hi, Ellie, it's me," Gina answered, peeking into the room.

The little girl's eyes lit up as soon as she heard Gina's voice.

"Gina!" Ellie cried, overjoyed. And then her eyes shifted to what her uncle's friend was holding in her hands. "Did you bring me something?" she asked Gina eagerly.

"Ellie," Shane admonished. "What did I tell you about asking that?"

Ellie dropped her head. "Not to," she mumbled in reply.

Gina pretended not to pay attention to the exchange between Shane and his niece.

"Of course I brought you something," she told Ellie, walking into the family room. "I brought you chicken soup."

Ellie's face fell. "Oh." Then, because her uncle had made it clear how important manners were, the little girl politely said, "Thank you."

Wow, Gina thought, clearly impressed. Shane should be giving parenting lessons.

Ellie was still staring hopefully at what Gina was holding in her hands. Not wanting to prolong the torture a second longer, Gina said, "And when you're finished eating your chicken soup, I brought you these comic books to read."

Ellie's forehead wrinkled, conveying that the little girl was slightly confused by the term she'd used. "Comic books?" Ellie repeated.

Gina sat down on the edge of the sofa, facing Ellie. "Comic books," she repeated, holding up one as a visual aid. It was a copy of the adventures of a band of friendly dogs who helped people. "See?"

Clapping her hands together, Ellie squealed her thanks, then she took the comic book from Gina. "This is for me?" she asked hopefully.

"All yours," Gina assured her.

Ellie's eyes crinkled as she leaned forward and hugged Gina. "Thank you!"

Looking on, Shane realized that he was still holding the basket Gina had brought.

"I'd better put this in the kitchen and get a couple of bowls. Three bowls," he amended, correcting himself.

"Three?" Gina questioned. Was he entertaining? Had she come at a bad time?

"Sure. You're going to have some with us, aren't you?" Shane asked.

"There's not all that much soup," Gina pointed out. "And I made it for you."

"Stay and have some," Shane urged her.

She didn't want Shane to feel obligated to share it with her, but she wasn't about to argue over it either. After all, this was what she secretly wanted. To become part of his life again and he part of hers. Ten years had passed since they'd been together but all that meant was that she had a loss of ten years to make up for.

"Can I help?" she called out.

He didn't answer her. Instead, he came back a couple of minutes later carrying a tray with three servings of soup and three spoons. He set the tray down on the coffee table that was right next to Ellie's sofa.

"I'm perfectly capable of ladling out three bowls of chicken soup," he told Gina.

"Of course you are," Gina replied. "I just like to help, that's all."

He looked down at the bowls, then back up at her. "You already did," he told her quietly.

There was that warm feeling again, Gina thought, reveling in the way it washed over her.

All three of them had soup for lunch. Her appetite nudged, Ellie even had seconds, although her bowl was slightly smaller than theirs was.

Clearing the bowls away, Gina wound up reading the comic books she had brought out loud to Ellie. After she had finished reading all of them to the little girl, they went on to play a board game. Shane attempted to beg off, but Gina and Ellie ganged up on him and he had no choice but to agree to play, too.

He was a reluctant participant at first, but Gina watched his resistance dissolve when Ellie looked up at her uncle with her big, soulful eyes.

With a sigh, he murmured, "I can't say no to you." Triumphant, Ellie clapped her hands in delight.

After that, they played one game after another until, completely tired out, Ellie fell asleep with one of the characters they were using on the board game clutched in her hand.

Gina rose slowly, taking care not to wake the little girl. She waited until she had walked out of the room before she risked saying anything to Shane.

"That little girl has more energy than any three people I know," she told him.

Shane smiled fondly as he looked back at Ellie over his shoulder.

"I wish I could tap into that," he confided honestly. "Thanks for bringing the soup and the comic books. And for helping out today," he added.

"I didn't do anything out of the ordinary," Gina protested, although truthfully, she liked being on the receiving end of his gratitude.

"You kept her entertained," Shane pointed out. "Ellie was just about ready to jump out of her skin when you got here just like the cavalry."

"Then I'm glad I could help keep her in her skin," Gina teased, loving the warm feeling that was spreading all through her just because of the way he was looking at her. "That's a wonderful little girl you have there. You've done a great job raising her."

"Half the time I think she's just raising herself," he confided.

"Don't kid yourself. I can see you in her," Gina told him. "The way she holds her head when she's thinking. That crooked smile on her lips when she's about to spring a surprise. She even phrases things the way you do. There's a hint of a lisp, of course," she added with a grin, "but it's definitely you."

"You're imagining things," he told her.

"No, I'm just very good at observing things. And at remembering," Gina added.

Because the moment had gotten so serious, it made her a little uneasy. She was afraid of having any sort of a serious conversation with Shane, afraid of any recriminations he might bring up.

Clearing her throat, she turned away, saying, "I'd better get my picnic basket so you can take advantage of the moment and get some rest. Something tells me that ball of fire in the next room will wake up raring to go."

"You're probably right," he agreed. "It was all I could do to convince her to rest one more day. We compromised on the sofa, but she was about to abandon it when you came over."

In the kitchen, he took a look at the container she'd brought. It was less than half full.

Gina saw the way he was looking at it and guessed at what he was thinking. "No need to transfer anything. You just keep the container until Ellie finishes the soup. I will take back the basket, though."

"Hold on. I can't have you leave with an empty basket," he told her. He opened the refrigerator and rummaged around.

Because his back blocked her view, she didn't know what he was doing until he was finished taking things out and putting them into the basket. Shane closed the lid before he turned around so that she wasn't able to see what he was doing.

Curious, Gina opened up the basket and saw that Shane had put about half a dozen pastries into the basket, just like the ones he'd brought to the bridal shower.

She raised her eyes to look at him. "You want me to get fat, don't you?" she asked. Gina was only half-kidding.

"It'll take more than half a dozen pastries to make you fat," he told her.

"Maybe, but it's a good start." Debating, Gina made up her mind and pushed the basket back toward him. "I can't take these."

Shane didn't understand. He thought she liked them. "Why not?" he asked.

"Because Ellie might want to eat them." It certainly wasn't because she didn't like them.

"It's not like I can't make any more of them," he told Gina. He nodded at the pastries in her basket. "I was just practicing with these."

That didn't make any sense to her. "You have to practice?" she questioned.

"Sure. Concert pianists have to practice," Shane pointed out, then shrugged. "Chefs aren't any different."

"I never thought of it that way," Gina admitted. In her opinion, you couldn't improve on excellence.

The room felt as if it was getting smaller to her. And warmer. Gina realized that somehow, Shane was standing closer to her than he had been a few moments ago.

Or maybe she was the one who was closer to him than she had been before.

However the logistics had gone, the end result was that her skin was beginning to tingle and desire was firing up within her like a newly lit display of fireworks against the darkened sky.

Gina knew she was asking for trouble because things were going so smoothly, but she found herself wishing Shane would kiss her again the way he had yesterday in the parking lot.

Except longer this time.

And then, the next moment, she wasn't wishing any more.

Because he was.

Chapter Fourteen

Gina wasn't aware of the basket sliding from her limp fingers. All she knew was that her hands were now free to go around Shane's neck.

Her heart pounding, she threaded her arms around his neck. Rising up on her toes, Gina allowed herself to sink into the kiss, reveling in the heated sensations that were being released throughout her entire body.

Feeling suddenly incredibly hungry for more, Shane wrapped his arms around her, drawing Gina closer to him as he deepened the kiss. Just for a moment he lost himself not only in the kiss but in all the old, wonderfully familiar feelings that kissing Gina had once again brought back to him in all their vivid glory.

He could have sworn that those feelings had all died long ago, lying buried in some forgotten grave where broken dreams went to die. Yet here they were back again, just as strong as ever.

Stronger.

Feeling insatiable, Shane slanted his mouth over and over against hers, each kiss deeper and full of more longing than the last.

Heaven help him, he wanted her, wanted to recapture all those emotions that had once pulsed so vividly between them.

Shane's heart quickened as his pulse raced faster and faster. And then, from some deep, distant nether region, common sense pushed its way to the foreground. Strengthening, it took hold of him.

With effort, he drew his head back and slid his hands from her waist up to her shoulders. Exercising extreme control, he held her away from him.

"I should get back to Ellie," he said, his voice tight, hoarse.

"Right," Gina heard herself agreeing.

Her brain caught up half a beat later. What had she been thinking, kissing him like that? It wasn't as if she could lure him into making love with her, not with his niece sleeping in the family room and liable to wake up at any second.

"You can't leave her alone," she said, embarrassed that for a few moments, she hadn't been thinking of Ellie, only of how it had once been for Shane and her. "Go," she urged him, waving him toward the family room. "And thanks for the pastries," she added belatedly. Her brain was having a lot of difficulty processing what had just happened out here to her.

"Thanks for the soup—and the comic books," he added with a smile that quickly burrowed straight into her chest.

She nodded, reluctant to see Shane leave despite what she'd just said about his going to his niece.

"Don't mention it. And please let me know if there's anything else you need," Gina added. She was stalling and she knew it.

C'mon, Gina, get those feet moving toward your car. Go home.

"I will," Shane told her.

The look in his eyes told her more than that, but Gina was afraid that she was letting her imagination read far too much into it.

Shane had kissed her, she thought, kissed her the way he used to, with abandoned passion, and that was enough for now, she told herself.

She could build on that.

Gina didn't remember driving home. Didn't remember walking from her car into her apartment. All she was aware of the entire time she was going from here to there was the golden glow that was radiating within her.

The golden glow began to dissipate the second she saw the light blinking on her landline. Someone had left her a message. It was probably Sylvie calling with another mini-emergency for her to handle. Gina closed her eyes. She was certainly earning her money with that one.

Why hadn't Sylvie called her on her cell? Gina wondered, opening her eyes again. Oh well, she'd find out soon enough.

Sighing, she kicked off her shoes, got comfortable and played the single message on the phone.

She stiffened the moment she heard the voice. It wasn't Sylvie calling her, it was her mother.

"Hi, Gina. Haven't heard from you for a while now. Just checking to see how you are. I'll talk to you later."

Gina sighed again, louder this time.

Her five-foot-two mother was the only person in her world who could say those words—"I'll talk to you later"—and make them sound like a threat.

She pressed her lips together, thinking. Just as she was debating whether or not to call her mother back—"not" was winning—the landline rang. Caller ID identified the number as belonging to Anna Bongino.

"Not really the patient type, are you, Mom?" she murmured to the telephone.

Gina knew that if she didn't pick up the receiver, she was fairly certain that her mother would have the police dragging the nearby lake for her body. Taking a deep breath, she brought the receiver up to her ear.

Summoning a cheerful voice from somewhere deep within, Gina said, "Hi, Mom."

"Hello yourself, Gina," her mother responded. Gina knew something was off immediately. "I just thought I'd call and ask what's new in your life."

And that confirmed it. She knew that all-too-innocent tone of voice. Rather than beat around the bush and try to feel her mother out, she went straight to the question at the heart of this call.

"You know, don't you?" she accused.

"Know what, Gina?" Anna asked, taking her innocent tone up an octave.

Gina rolled her eyes. Her mother knew. Knew about Shane suddenly reappearing in her life. This was all her own fault. She should have never said anything to her sister.

"Mom," she said, doing her best to see the funny side

rather than lose her temper, "your abilities as an actress really leave a great deal to be desired."

Rather than become defensive, Anna merely said, "I'm sure I have no idea what you're referring to, Gina."

She wasn't about to drop this. "Yes, you do," Gina responded. "You're calling me because you're hoping to pump me for information about Shane."

"Shane?" Anna repeated so innocently Gina almost believed her, emphasis on "almost."

"Do you mean that really nice boy from college who would have made such a wonderful husband for you? *That* Shane?" she asked.

And now she oversold it, Gina thought. "Yes, Mother," she replied, at the end of her patience. "*That* Shane."

"Are you telling me that he's back? He's here in Bedford?" Anna cried.

Gina sighed. "Still not cutting it as an actress, Mom."

Ignoring her daughter's sarcasm, Anna plowed ahead. "When? How? Are you seeing him again?" her mother asked with enough enthusiasm to make Gina harbor a sliver of doubt, just enough to give the woman the benefit of possibly not knowing about this supposed "happy" development in her life.

"Slow down, Mom," she cautioned. "Oddly enough, I ran into him while helping my latest client with all her wedding requests."

There was silence on the other end of the line. Eerie silence. And then her mother almost wailed, "Don't tell me he's the groom."

Okay, maybe her mother really *was* on the level, she thought. "No, Mom, Shane actually 'creates' wedding cakes. That's how I 'ran into' him. My client sent me to him to ask that he do her wedding cake. It seems that Shane is very much in demand."

She heard her mother chuckle. "I'll bet," Anna interjected. "So, did you talk? Did you catch up on old times?"

She really wished that her mother would drop this. "It's not that easy, Mom."

"Of course it is," Anna insisted. "Talking was always easy for you. You said your first sentence when you were nine months old," she said proudly.

Gina closed her eyes. "So you've told me, Mom," she said wearily. "But this takes a little more finesse than that."

Anna seemed to be unfazed by her daughter's protest. "So? You've had thirty-two years of practice. Finesse already," Anna urged. Then, before her daughter could say anything she wouldn't welcome hearing, Anna went on with her sales pitch. "He really was such a very nice young man. Maybe I should invite the two of you over for dinner sometime."

And so it starts, Gina thought. Maybe she could put the skids on her mother's plan, at least for now. "You'd have to set three places at the table."

"You don't want your father there?" Anna questioned, confused. "I know he can be irritating at times, but still, he's your—"

"No, Mom, that's not it," Gina protested, stopping her mother before this got completely out of hand. "I'm saying that you'd need to set three *extra* places if you invite us over."

Her mother was quiet for a moment again. Then, in almost a hushed voice, unhappy voice, she asked, "Shane has a wife?"

She should have just taken her chances and not answered, Gina thought. "No, Mom, he has a four-year-old niece. And before you ask, he's her guardian."

"Oh my lord, he's even nicer than he used to be," her mother enthused.

Okay, she knew her mother meant well, but this was just agitating her at this point. "I've got to go, Mom. I've got a lot of details to see to if this wedding is going to be a success."

"Let me know how it's going!" She could hear her mother's voice practically radiating from the receiver as she started to hang it up.

"If there's anything to report," Gina replied and then quickly disconnected the call before her mother had a chance to say anything further that was just going to annoy her.

Gina took a deep breath, willing herself to get her agitation under control. She really couldn't blame her mother for being like this and taking up Shane's cause. Shane had charmed the woman from the first moment her mother had laid eyes on him.

Same as her, Gina thought.

Although she tried to will herself to go to sleep, she just couldn't seem to manage it.

Gina had finally managed to drop off to sleep when her alarm went off. The shrill alarm mingled with the sound of her ringing cell phone. Bleary-eyed, she reached for the alarm clock, shut it off and glanced at the time.

Seven o'clock.

By her calculation, she had gotten under five hours' sleep. Lord, she hoped she didn't look it, she thought.

Pulling herself together, she reached for the cell phone and brought it up close to her face.

"Hello?" she mumbled into what she hoped was the right end of the cell phone.

"I'm sorry, did I just wake you up?" she heard Shane apologize.

Her eyes flew open. Instantly, she could feel her brain scrambling in a frantic attempt to focus itself. She dragged air deep into her lungs, praying that would do the trick.

"No, I'm up," she protested, then repeated, "I'm up. I've been up for hours."

"Your voice doesn't sound like it," Shane told her.

Gina sighed. "That's because I'm lying," she admitted. "I had trouble falling asleep last night." Then, realizing what that had to sound like to him—that she was telling him that he was the reason she couldn't sleep—she quickly said, "My mother called when I got in and, well, you know how she is."

"Charming, as I recall," he answered with an amused laugh.

"No," she contradicted. "That's just my mother's gentleman caller facade. Her real persona is a lot different," Gina insisted. Not wanting to go into any further explanations about the woman—or what they'd discussed—Gina changed the subject back to the reason that he had called her in the first place. "What can I do for you?"

Shane got down to business. "I usually do a trial-run cake before I create the actual one for the wedding," he told her. "And since you told me that the bride was being extremely careful about not eating anything that she feels might make her gain weight, I was wondering if you'd like to be her stand-in."

All sorts of ideas ran through Gina's head, none of which really made any sense to her in this particular context.

"Excuse me?"

"What I'm asking you is if you would like to come in and sample the wedding cake I'm creating for Sylvie? Provided that you're not too busy," Shane added. He sounded completely serious.

"I'm never too busy for you—um, for your cake," she managed to amend at the last minute. "When would you like me to come by your shop?"

"How does two o'clock sound?"

Perfect. But then, any time he would have suggested would have been perfect, she thought.

"I'll be there," she answered brightly. "How's Ellie doing?" she asked, wondering if the little girl was still sick.

"Great," he answered. "She bounced up out of bed early this morning like she was never sick."

"I told you," Gina said, pleased.

"You did," Shane acknowledged, "and deep down inside, I knew you were right, but I still couldn't help worrying."

"That's because you're a good dad, I mean good uncle," she corrected herself.

"Actually," Shane confided to her, "a lot of times I feel as if I'm both an uncle *and* a father to that little girl."

There were a thousand things Gina wanted to say to him. She came very close to blurting out that her mother had asked about him, but she felt she was still in uncharted territory. That meant that she needed to be as cautious as possible so as not to endanger any progress that might have been made so far. She was intent on building things up between them, not in having them disintegrate.

So Gina curbed her desire to say all sorts of positive, possibly over-the-top things to him and just went with something relatively neutral.

"There should be a way to hyphenate that in your case," she told him. "You know, like Uncle-Dad."

He laughed. "Like that's not going to confuse Ellie at all."

Gina grew serious. "Does she know what happened to her parents?"

"Yes. I told her the first time she asked about them. I put it in terms she could understand—that Mommy and Daddy had been in an accident and they went straight up to heaven to keep God company. That seemed to satisfy her at the time. She doesn't feel that they abandoned her if that's what you're asking."

"No, I wasn't thinking of that," Gina said honestly. "After all, she's only four."

"A very bright, precocious four," Shane pointed out. "She certainly keeps me on my toes."

"Oh, I'll bet." She could listen to the sound of his voice against her ear all day, but she knew he had work to do. Just as she knew she needed to let him get to it. "All right then, I'll see you at two—unless you call and tell me that you want me there later."

"No, two will be fine. Unless the stove blows up. I'm kidding," Shane assured her when he heard silence on the other end. "That hasn't happened to me for a while now."

"You're still kidding, right?" Gina asked uncertainly.

"Actually, it was this ancient stove that I used when

I was in Uganda and no, I'm not," he told her. "It really did blow up."

"Okay, my cue to leave," she said. She knew that if she didn't force herself to hang up now, she never would. "Bye."

"Goodbye, Gina."

The sound of his voice echoed in her head for the rest of the morning, keeping her company and whispering of things that were to come.

Maybe.

Chapter Fifteen

"You look exhausted."

It wasn't what Shane had intended to say to Gina when he saw her walking into his shop that afternoon at exactly two o'clock on the dot, but her wearied appearance caught him totally by surprise.

Gina swept into the shop and went straight toward one of the two tables in the showroom. "Flatterer," she quipped, dropping her shoulder bag on the table.

"No, I'm serious." Shane came around the counter and joined the woman on the other side. He searched her face. "Is everything all right?"

"It is now—I think," she replied uncertainly.

"And before?" he asked, waiting to hear the explanation behind why she looked as if she'd been on a forced march for the last eighteen hours.

She sighed. "Before it was like being in a canoe, paddling madly while trying to navigate in the middle of a torrential storm."

Shane pulled out a chair, silently urging her to sit down. He waited until she did, then he dropped into the one opposite her before he said, "You are going to translate that into English so that the rest of us can understand, right?"

She sighed. She supposed she was carrying on a little bit too much, but she had earned it after what she'd gone through.

"I can't wait until this wedding is over with," she told him with a sigh.

He got up and poured her a cup of tea from the stand he had set up to the side for his customers. "I kind of thought it might have something to do with that. What happened?" he asked.

She looked up at him with a smile. "Well, aside from my having to sweet-talk a wedding cake from the much sought after 'Cassidy'—which turned out to be a good thing," she quickly added, "and finding a contractor who could repair an unexpected large gaping hole in the church roof in time for the wedding, not to mention securing a decent photographer to replace the one who suddenly remembered he had a conflict—two weddings at the same time taking place in opposite directions— I just spent the whole morning negotiating with a florist who tried to tell me that carnations made a better statement decorating the church than the lilies that the bride wanted."

She paused to take a sip of the tea, then sighed as the hot liquid curled its way through her system. "I had no idea that florists could be so temperamental and hard-nosed."

Listening, Shane nodded and looked properly sympathetic.

"Who won?" he asked when she paused to take another breath.

About to take another sip of tea, Gina raised her eyes up over the rim of the cup. Her eyes met his. "Who do you think?"

Shane laughed. "I don't have to think, I know. You always were persuasive," he recalled fondly. She really did look wiped out, though, he thought. "Look, if you want to go home and unwind, we can do this tomorrow. There's no huge rush."

"I *am* unwinding," Gina informed him. Being here with him like this was having an oddly tranquilizing effect on her, she realized. She had gotten past the tense, nervous stage with him, so that was a good thing. "Right now, what I need most is a friendly face." She smiled at him. "You qualify."

Setting the small delicate cup back in its saucer, she looked around the showroom. It was just the two of them out front, although she did hear the sounds of activity coming from the back area where all the baking was done.

"Where's Ellie?" Gina asked him. "I expected to see her out here."

He could see why she would have thought that, given what he'd told her about why he had gone into this line of work to begin with.

"I needed to concentrate this morning so I gave Ellie a choice of going to preschool or staying home with Barbara," he said, referring to Ellie's nanny. "She picked Barbara—big surprise."

Gina put her own interpretation to his explanation. "Ellie doesn't like going to school?"

"Ellie loves learning new things well enough—as a matter of fact, she likes reading her storybooks to me. What she doesn't like is having to follow rules. She finds them 'not fun,'" he said, quoting his niece. "I guess she thinks they're too confining."

"Wonder where she gets that from," Gina said, doing her best not to laugh. She didn't succeed.

He looked at Gina in surprise. "Hey, I followed rules."

"Funny, I seem to remember you cutting classes and talking me into cutting them, too, so that we could spend the afternoon just hanging out together."

Shane shrugged. "That was a unique set of circumstances," he told her. "And besides, I was a kid then."

"You were twenty," Gina reminded him. "And Ellie's only four," she added as if that explained why the little girl was acting rebelliously in his eyes.

"Oh, but at four I listened to the adults in my life."

"I wouldn't know," Gina replied. "I didn't know you when you were four. You could have been a hellion at that age," she teased.

"Well, I wasn't," he told her. "I was a quiet, mousy kid back then. Ellie's nothing like that," Shane pointed out. And then he looked concerned. "Ellie's so smart for her age, there are times she sounds like an adult trapped in a little person's body. She worries me," he confessed. "There is such a thing as being too smart."

He was serious, Gina realized and tried to reassure him. "Not if she has someone looking out for her, guiding her."

"You're talking about me," he concluded.

"No, I'm talking about my imaginary friend, Sam," Gina said, gesturing about at the empty air. "Of course I'm talking about you. Hey, you're kind, patient, creative and have a very level head on your shoulders. If you ask me, I'd say that Ellie's future couldn't be in more excellent hands."

Shane waved her words away. "There's no need to flatter me, Gina. I've already agreed to create this cake for your client's wedding."

She was insulted that Shane thought she would do that. "I'm not flattering you," she said with an edge in her voice. "I'm telling it like it is."

Shane raised a brow, looking at her. She could feel herself squirming inside. She always did whenever Shane looked at her that way.

He was getting to her and she needed to hold it together. She didn't want him feeling that she was coming on to him in his workplace. Shane had kissed her, and she'd kissed him back. Twice. He had to know how she felt about him. The next move was up to him and she had a feeling it wouldn't happen here, in his place of work. Not with his people only a few steps away in the back. They were liable to walk in at any second.

"You said something about sampling the wedding cake you created," Gina prompted, looking toward the back where she assumed he had it.

"Right." He rose again, nodding toward the back area. "It's in the back. Let me go get it."

"I'll be here," she told him cheerfully.

The second Shane left, she whipped out her small mirror from her purse and quickly looked herself over. Gina winced. He was right. She looked as if she'd been fighting off dragons for the last forty-eight hours. Damage control involved doing a quick pass through her hair with her comb and freshening up her fading lipstick.

She barely finished the latter when she heard Shane returning to the showroom.

Throwing the lipstick back into her purse, she deliberately straightened in her chair as if assuming better posture helped somehow.

Gina thought she would just be sampling a slice of cake. She wasn't prepared for what he brought out. It was a complete, detailed miniature wedding cake like the one he proposed to make for the actual event.

Nor did she expect to be totally blown away by it. The cake was comprised of five tiny tiers, arranged to look like wedding gifts piled one on top of another. The "gifts" came with ribbons made out of what she assumed was intricately decorated icing. There was also a cascade of pink roses, also made out of icing, spilling down one side of the "gifts."

Visually, it was incredible.

"It's beautiful," Gina whispered to him in utter awe. "A total feast for the eyes," she added, looking up at Shane.

"All right, so it looks good," he responded. "But the true test here is how it tastes." Cutting a slice of off-white chiffon cake for her from the bottom, he slid it onto a plate. She noted that the filling had cherries in it. Shane handed the plate to her along with a fork. "Tell me what you think."

"What I think is that it's a sin to cut up such a work of art and put it into my mouth," she told him honestly.

"Then you'd be missing out on the best part—provided that everything turned out the way it should," Shane added. He nodded toward the plate. "Tell me what you think," he repeated.

"I think you could give humble lessons to the florist," Gina responded.

"Not interested in the florist," he told her, dismissing the man. "I'm interested in what you think of the cake."

She expected to like the cake. After all, she had already had some of his pastries—more than she should have, she knew, but they were very difficult to resist. She assumed the same would be true of the cake Shane had created for Sylvie's wedding. It would be delicious.

Delicious was a paltry word in this case.

The moment she slid the fork into her mouth, Gina knew that the bar of her expectations had been set much too low. This was by far better than anything she had thought it would be. There was an explosion of magnificent taste in her mouth.

She sat there, taking in a deep breath as she savored what was in her mouth.

"Well?" Shane prodded gently when she hadn't said anything.

Gina looked at him. Rather than answer, she took another forkful and put it into her mouth. Her lips closed over it, savoring the exquisitely seductive dance that was occurring on her tongue.

She swallowed and smiled. "What I think is that you are *definitely* in the right business. I also think that my tongue is in love." She eyed her plate, tempted to stuff the rest of it into her mouth. It took effort to restrain herself. "Where did you *ever* learn how to do this?"

He shrugged dismissively at the implied compliment. "You can't help picking up things along the way if you keep your ears open. So, you really like it?" Shane asked again, just in case Gina thought she had to be nice and wasn't being totally straightforward.

"Like it?" Gina repeated. "This cake is a whole new reason to get married."

The second the words were out of her mouth, she realized what she had said and the memories that those words could very well have unearthed.

Idiot!

Clearing her throat, Gina tried to walk her words back. "I mean—"

Shane held up his hand to stop the apology he knew was coming before she could attempt to form the words for it.

"That's all right, Gina, I know what you meant. Thanks." He smiled. "It's good to know you liked it."

"You don't need me to verify your efforts," she told him. "You know you're good."

"I know I *try* to be good. But there have been failures. And just because something works for me doesn't mean that it's going to work for someone else—visually or taste-wise," he added.

"So I'm your test guinea pig?" Gina asked with a laugh.

"I wouldn't exactly refer to you as that," Shane told her. "But I can't very well ask anyone who works for me to give me their 'honest' opinion because I sense that they're afraid if I don't like what they say, I'll terminate them."

He wasn't like that and she knew it, but she decided to tease him a little. The situation had grown far too serious. "Would you?"

"Of course not," Shane told her with feeling, and then shrugged. "But you can't change the way people think. And anyway, what I wanted was the opinion of someone who had it in them to be brutally honest—like you."

Gina blew out a breath. The remark stung. She hadn't expected that. But there was no sense in getting defensive about his comment, even though it really bothered her that that was the way Shane thought about her.

"I guess I had that coming," she allowed.

Shane saw the look on her face. He'd said too much, he thought.

"I didn't mean it that way," he told her. "I meant that you're not afraid of saying what you think."

She drew back her shoulders, unconsciously bracing herself for what might be coming. "I've also learned that saying the first thing that pops into my head is something that I had to temper because it wasn't always what I really *wanted* to say." Her eyes met his. "I did pay a price for that. I think I already told you that."

She needed to leave, Gina thought. Now, because she was afraid that she might say something she was going to regret again. Either that, or just break down in tears. Neither was something she wanted Shane to see or hear.

Gina rose to her feet then. Picking up her purse, she slid the strap onto her shoulder, securing the purse with a tug.

"Your wedding cake exceeds any expectation I had and I'm sure that Sylvie will say the same thing. Don't change a thing—about the cake," she emphasized, looking at him pointedly.

Shane silently upbraided himself. The tight rein he had kept on his emotions while being around Gina all this time had slipped and he had allowed those hurt feelings he'd been suppressing all this time to come spilling out. And he didn't feel any better by doing it; he just felt worse.

"Gina—" he began, trying to find a way to apologize for allowing his pettiness to take over.

She was already at the entrance, one hand on the

doorknob. All she wanted to do was get away. "I forgot I promised the bride I'd see her today and give her a progress report on everything."

He knew that was an excuse. Shane tried again. "Gina—"

The corners of her eyes were stinging. She had to get out of there before she broke down. She kept her face averted.

"I'll give her a five-and-a-half-star rating out of five for your cake. That'll make her very happy," she told Shane as she hurried out the door.

Moving quickly, Gina got into her car. She slammed the door just as she heard Shane coming out of his shop. He was coming for her.

Gina gunned the engine. He was going to try to apologize, or maybe say that one bad turn deserved another, she didn't know. In either case, she didn't want to hear it.

Most of all, she didn't want to let him see her crying. Crying was a sign of weakness and she had sworn to herself that she wasn't going to be weak. Not ever again. She'd made her apologies and he really hadn't taken her at her word.

Fine. She needed to move on now.

No matter how much she wanted to be with him, her rejection—her stupidly worded, baseless rejection—would always be there between them and he was never going to let her forget it.

Well, what was done was done and she was through trying to atone for it.

It was time to forget about him.

Chapter Sixteen

It had been a long, grueling day. At one point, Gina didn't think that it would ever come to an end. She'd even seriously entertained the idea of throwing up her hands and quitting, but in her heart she knew she couldn't do that. Quitting would have gone against everything that she was.

But she had to admit that the idea was nonetheless awfully tempting.

Sylvie had needed a great deal of hand-holding today. Her latest client had gotten into an argument with her maid of honor last night and hurt feelings were still very much alive and well today. Monica had actually threatened to hand in her title and her gown and be a no-show at the wedding.

The cause of the argument was so petty, Gina couldn't even get the two women to talk about it. Nevertheless, through sheer grit Gina had managed to get them to patch things up. It had taken her the better part of four hours to smooth things out and to get the two women to call a truce. She embarrassed them into realizing that they would be sacrificing one of the most important days in not just Sylvie's life, but in Monica's, as well.

"Mine?" Monica cried in a shrill voice. "How can it be mine?"

"Because not everyone gets to be asked to be a maid of honor," Gina informed the woman in a voice that bordered on no-nonsense. "There's a lot of unspoken love that goes into making that choice. You don't want to allow an inconsequential argument to make you lose sight of that, do you?"

Using that, and similar arguments, Gina managed to intimidate both women into calling a truce.

After she got the two women to grudgingly agree with her, they wound up crying and made up. And then Sylvie and Monica *celebrated* making up. Gina, being instrumental in making them resolve their differences, perforce had to remain for that part, as well. The women had insisted on it.

It was close to eight o'clock by the time Gina was finally able to pull into her parking spot. Getting out of her car, she crossed the parking lot and made her way to her ground-floor apartment.

She didn't see Shane sitting in front of her door until she was almost on top of him. By then it was too late for her to retreat unnoticed.

He had obviously been waiting for her for a while now. The second he saw her, Shane scrambled to his feet, his body partially blocking access to her door.

Gina's fingers tightened around her keys, momentarily at a loss as to what to do. She raised her chin defensively. "What are you doing here?"

"Waiting for you." Shane was tempted to leave it at that, but that didn't begin to explain what had forced him to come here in the first place. So he told her the truth and completed his answer. "Thinking of all the different ways to tell you I'm sorry."

No, damn it! She wasn't going to allow herself to let him into her life again. She'd finally talked herself into putting him out of her thoughts. She couldn't go back to square one again.

Why was he doing this to her?

But he was just standing there, looking at her. Waiting for her to say something.

Almost grudgingly, Gina asked in a stilted voice, "Where's Ellie?"

"She's home," he answered. His smile was self-deprecating. "I asked Barbara to watch her at double her rate. When I got to triple, she was more than happy to accommodate me and stay. Even told me to take all the time I needed." Shane's expression turned serious as he looked at her. "I figured I'd need a lot of time." He searched her face, looking for some indication that he had some small, slight chance of making amends. He nodded at the door. "Gina, can I come in?"

She knew she should say no. Knew she should tell Shane that they had nothing to talk about and just send him on his way.

Turning from Shane she almost said it, almost told him to go.

But then she unlocked her door and walked into her apartment. She left the door standing open behind her.

He took the open door as consent on her part. Grateful, he walked into the apartment behind her.

Easing the door closed once he'd crossed the threshold, Shane repeated his apology. "I'm sorry that things got out of hand today. I didn't mean for them to—"

Gina swung around to face him. Her face was a collage of all the mixed emotions churning within her. "You've been back in Bedford, what, three years now?" she asked, cutting into his apology.

"Yes," he replied, never taking his eyes off her face.

He saw anger creasing Gina's forehead as she asked him in an accusatory voice, "Why didn't you look me up when you came home?"

"I didn't think you wanted me to," he explained haplessly.

"You didn't know *what* I was thinking," she countered. "You never gave me the option of telling you." She was struggling to keep contained the anger that had been unearthed in the aftermath of what had happened in his shop today.

She could actually feel it growing, swelling in her chest. Seeking release.

He needed to phrase this right, Shane thought, searching for the right words. He didn't want this to turn into another argument. He hadn't come here for that. He'd come for forgiveness.

"Maybe it hasn't really occurred to you yet, but by the time I came back, my whole situation had changed. It wasn't just me anymore. I was responsible for the care and welfare of a little human being. I was then and I am now," he emphasized. "And I felt that if you didn't want me when I was alone, I *knew* you wouldn't want me with a little kid to raise. I couldn't stand to hear you turn me down again."

Gina had fisted her hands on her hips, her eyes flashing not just at what Shane had said but at the terrible waste that had been created because of all the miscommunication that had gone down.

Not to mention all the time they had lost because of the thoughtless rejection that she had said to him in fear.

"Sorry, smart guy," Gina informed him, "but you were wrong. You didn't know anything." Tossing her head, her eyes narrowed as she said, "I would have loved to have been there to raise that little girl with you."

He didn't believe her. "You're only saying that."

She threw up her hands, uttering an unintelligible noise in her sheer frustration. "How do I get you to believe me? Should I get all three of our names tattooed somewhere on my body, linked in hearts? What?" she demanded. "Tell me what to do and I'll do it!"

The corners of Shane's mouth curved. "I admit that would be interesting," he acknowledged.

She stared at him, shaking her head. She didn't know what to think.

Was he being sweet? Did she drop her guard and believe him, or was he waiting for that so he could get back at her for what he felt she'd put him through with that rejection years ago?

She didn't know and she was afraid of making the wrong choice.

"Damn you, Shane," she cried, "you're the only one who's ever made me crazy like this."

"Oh no," he contradicted. He was grinning at her now and the grin was working its way into her system, seducing her. "I can't take credit for that. You were this way long before I ever came along. A 'self-made woman' I think was the way you once referred to yourself."

Exasperated, not to mention frustrated, Gina doubled up her fist and swung it back, ready to punch him in her agitation.

Shane caught her hand, blocked the punch and pulled her to him.

Pinning Gina's arms against her sides, he brought his mouth down to hers and kissed her. Kissed her long and hard, until she stopped struggling and kissed him back.

Her hands loosened, no longer fisted, she raised them up and threaded her arms around his neck as the kiss continued growing in intensity and depth.

Gina sighed as Shane drew his lips away. "I don't want to fight, Gina," he told her softly.

Her mouth slowly curved into a smile. "Oh, I don't know," she responded. "Wrestling's got some things going for it."

But he shook his head. "Me, I always liked that old slogan from the sixties. Make love, not war." He grew serious as he searched her face, wanting to make sure that he hadn't misjudged the situation. "Make love with me, Gina," he urged in a low, seductive voice. "It's all I've thought about for the last ten years."

Gina paused and for one awful moment, he thought she was going to turn him down. That she was going to tell him that they had lost their chance and shouldn't reopen old wounds.

And then, her eyes locked on his, she whispered, "Prove it."

That was when he finally knew that it was going to be all right. That they had both paid for his rash proposal and her equally as rash refusal.

"With pleasure," he answered, pressing his lips against her throat. He felt the pulse there jump in response and the desire he'd felt building within him increased tenfold.

Holding himself in check despite the fact that he ached to take her right then and there, Shane made slow, deliberate love to every inch of her body, causing Gina to yield to him as he crisscrossed her skin with a network of hot, ardent kisses, branding her body everywhere he touched.

Making it his.

Shane only vaguely remembered stripping Gina's clothes from her body.

What left a far greater imprint on his brain was feeling her fingers traveling along his chest, his shoulders, his torso. Touching him everywhere.

Arousing him to an incredible degree.

Every time her hand passed over another part of his body, Shane could feel himself responding to her, feel himself aching and wanting her the way he had never wanted another woman before.

Because in his soul, he knew that he had never loved another woman, not the way he loved her. Even while he kept denying it to himself over the years, he knew he loved Gina.

Always had.

Always would, Shane now thought silently. Even if all he ever would have was this one night with her, he knew himself well enough to know that he would never love anyone else the soul-branding way that he loved the woman here with him now.

A white-hot passion wrapped itself around Shane as

he blanketed Gina's body with a burning array of kisses, spreading them all up and down her heaving skin.

He had her back pressed against the sofa cushions when Gina surprised him by suddenly pulling him to her, reversing their positions. Determined to return the favor. Pressing her mouth against his throat, his shoulders, his chest, Gina all but devoured him, startled by the amount of passion that had been unleashed within her. Every place she touched became a burning, erotic area, moist and throbbing. Desire just continued mounting and she acted on it.

Because he could hold himself in check for only so long when she did that, Shane flipped their positions again, laying her on her back. From there he began to anoint all the regions of her body, working his way from her mouth to the hollow of her throat, down her breasts, then on to her quivering belly.

She thought he would stop there and she tried to wrap her legs around his torso, arching against him. But he was too quick for her.

His mouth went questing farther and farther, until, before she realized it, his tongue was mining the very core of her.

Gina suddenly arched her back, seized by an exquisite sensation that exploded within her. It sent shockwaves to every nether region.

Stunned, she stared at Shane, her heart pounding from the climax she'd just experienced.

She had no time to regroup because Shane began to move up along her body again, following his journey in reverse until the face that had filled so many of her dreams was looming right over hers.

Shane slipped his fingers through hers, joining them before he moved her legs apart with his knee.

Breathing hard, she pressed up against him, silently inviting him in.

"Look at me," he whispered.

Until that second, she hadn't realized that her eyes were closed. She opened them and that was when he entered her, creating one unit out of two.

Her heart was pounding wildly and she heard herself telling him, "I've missed this."

She thought she heard Shane say, "So have I," but she wasn't sure. Adrenaline was racing through her whole body, the rush she was experiencing blocking out everything except for the two of them and the myriad desires and passions throbbing demandingly throughout her entire being.

Shane began to move, slowly at first despite the urgency that propelled him. Gina matched each move he made, going faster and faster the second he did until it became a race to see which of them would be gratified first.

It was a tie.

Shane brought her up and over the summit of sensations just as it exploded all around him.

Euphoria showered down all around them, embracing them in its grip. Gina held on to it for as long as she could, trying to push the wave of pending sorrow as far back as she could.

It came anyway. Sorrow because the euphoria had receded.

But he was still there, still lying next to her, with his arm wrapped around her, holding her close. It pushed back the darkness. She listened as Shane's heart beat against hers, slowly returning back to its normal rhythmic beat.

She was afraid to move, afraid if she did, she would wind up chasing away all these delicious feelings, sending them back into some deep, dark cave where she couldn't reach them, couldn't touch them.

Gina felt him shifting, but Shane wasn't getting up. Instead, he just raised his head and pressed a soft kiss against her hair.

"You're awfully quiet," he commented. "Something wrong?"

She laughed at his question, at first softly and then with growing gusto until the sound echoed throughout the room.

"Wrong?" Gina repeated, raising her head so that she could look at his face. "For the first time in ten years, everything is absolutely right."

"Oh," he said and she could have sworn she heard relief in his voice. And then he confirmed it by saying, "You had me worried there for a minute. I thought maybe you were having regrets."

"Regrets?" she questioned.

"Yes, over what we just did," Shane elaborated.

"Regrets," she repeated as if it was a strange, foreign word that she was trying to make sense of. And then she laughed again. "My only regret is that it took so long for this to happen again."

Before he had a chance to comment on her words, Gina proceeded to take the lead so she could show him how much she didn't regret what had just happened there between them. She pushed him back against the sofa as she kissed every square inch of him, a prelude to another round of lovemaking.

Chapter Seventeen

Gina felt gloriously exhausted. She and Shane had made love two more times that evening. That was a total of three times, and she was amazed that she could still move. The temptation to curl up in Shane's arms and fall asleep was almost overwhelming. But Gina knew that she couldn't in good conscience give in to that.

That would be selfish, and she was determined not to ever put herself in the center of anything. Turning toward Shane, she murmured, "I'm going to get up and make you some fresh coffee."

"I'm not sure coffee will help," he told her, pulling her back into bed as she began to get up. "You have completely exhausted me."

"No, not for that," she laughed, brushing a quick kiss to his lips. "Coffee to wake you up so you don't drive off the side of the road while you're going home."

"I'm going home?" he asked.

"Yes. You want to be there in the morning when Ellie wakes up, don't you?"

He was surprised that she had even thought of the little girl. "And you're okay with that?" Shane questioned.

"Why wouldn't I be?" Gina asked. "She's not a rival, she's a sweet four-year-old girl—and your niece," she underscored. Funny how everything seemed to have changed now. "I think you wanting to be there for Ellie and take care of her is one of your more attractive qualities."

He would have been lying if he hadn't admitted that this was in the back of his head, wondering how all this was going to work out between them. "And you really don't mind my leaving to be with Ellie?"

"If you must know," she told him, pausing to give Shane one more quick kiss before slipping on a T-shirt to cover herself before she went to the kitchen, "right now I feel so absolutely wonderful, I think I could probably walk across water if I tried. Besides, I don't want to be the bad guy who keeps you away from Ellie." She made her way toward the doorway. "This way, you might be more inclined to maybe come back for seconds."

"Seconds and thirds and fourths," he added, calling after her as she left the room.

Gina smiled. That sounded good, but she wasn't about to hold him to what he had just said. Taking her opened coffee container out of the refrigerator, she measured out just enough to brew a superstrong mug of coffee the way she knew he liked it.

Setting the measuring spoon aside she poured a mugful of water into the machine. She wasn't going to allow herself to start dreaming about forever and risk being disappointed again. Once had been incredibly difficult for her. Twice would undoubtedly come close to killing her—or at least kill her spirit.

"Let's take it one day at a time and see where this goes," she told Shane as he came into the kitchen.

He had put his clothes on again and looked as if he was ready to leave. Well, that hadn't taken much persuading. She reminded herself that it had been her idea, so of course he was ready to go.

"Here's your coffee," she said, putting the mug on the table. "Why don't you sit down while you're having it," she coaxed.

Shane sat down and picked up the mug, looking at her thoughtfully. Gina was being cautious again, he thought. But he supposed, when he got right down to it, he couldn't really blame her. Not after the way things had gone down between them the first time. Granted, it had initially been her fault, yes, but he was the one who had taken it upon himself to go away. Looking back, he had to admit that had to have been hard on her.

He raised the mug, as if he was trying to toast something. "To one day at a time," he said, his eyes on Gina's.

He vowed to himself that he was going to tread lightly, but in the end, he was fully committed to convincing Gina that they belonged together. Whether she knew it or not, she had already passed the first hurdle. She had put Ellie ahead of not only herself, but also ahead of their rekindling romance.

It could only go well from here.

When Gina smiled at him after he'd made his "toast," he knew that he was on the right track.

Funny what reviving a romance could do for a person's spirit, Gina thought several days later. In her case,

it gave her the strength and fortitude to handle any cri-
sis and bear up to it all with surprising humor and an
astounding amount of energy.

Nothing daunted her.

Not even the fact that she had to deal with Sylvie
and her current client's never-ending cavalcade of mini-
emergencies.

This time Sylvie's newest emergency was courtesy
of the bride's pet cat, a calico named Cinnamon. Apparently, Cinnamon had managed to pull down Sylvie's
veil from where she had it hung up in the closet and then
the nimble cat proceeded to attack it in a frenzy, shred-
ding parts of it as if it were some sort of a gauzy enemy.

Reviewing the damage, Gina was temporarily speechless. But she was quick to rally—and in part she cred-
ited that to Shane's influence. She managed to calm
down the hysterical bride, then she told Sylvie that she
knew someone who could restore the veil to practically
its original state.

"You do?" Sylvie sniffled. "That would be nothing
short of a miracle. I had it handmade and flown in from
Switzerland."

Of course you did, Gina thought. "Trust me. I know
a miracle worker," Gina had told her, gathering up the
veil and depositing it into the large box it had origi-
nally come in.

Anna Bongino stared at the torn veil that Gina had
brought to her, then raised her eyes to her daughter's
face.

"Is this some sort of a joke, Gina?" she asked her
daughter.

"No, not a joke," Gina assured her, trying to sound

cheerful. "Think of it more as a challenge, Mom." She smiled at her mother. "I just talked you up to my latest client. You were a seamstress at that high-end bridal shop for twenty-three years, right, Mom?" Gina reminded her mother.

"Seamstress, yes. Miracle worker, no," Anna replied, taking the torn veil out of the box. She shook her head, totally astonished. "Besides, I took that job so that one day I would be able to sew your wedding dress and veil, not repair a veil that some girl's cat mistook for its dose of catnip."

Gina put her hand on her mother's arm. "Please, Mom. This means a lot to me."

Something had changed, Anna thought. She could *feel* it. She secretly blessed the woman she had sought out with her problem. She knew that Maizie and her friends were behind this. There was a lightness to her daughter that had been missing for years.

Looking at the veil again, Anna pretended to take a dim view of the veil's chances. She frowned, shaking her head. "I'll see what I can do, but I can't make any promises."

Gina threw her arms around her mother, totally surprising her. After a beat, Anna allowed herself to close her arms around her daughter and return the hug.

This was worth everything.

"You seem rather chipper, given that you're working with a crazy woman," Anna said. She couldn't resist adding, "Anything I should know about?"

"Nope, not a thing. I just love life, that's all," Gina answered as she began to leave. She paused at the door for a moment and said, "And for the record, I don't think of you as a crazy woman."

Anna drew back her shoulders. "I wasn't talking about me," she informed her daughter.

"I know." Gina laughed. "Thanks, Mom, you're a lifesaver. And I'll give you a call later to see how you're doing." She opened the front door, about to leave. "By the way, I'll need you to finish fixing the veil by Tuesday at the latest. Earlier if possible."

Anna's mouth dropped open, but she forced herself to swallow the first words that came to her. Instead, she just shook her head.

"It's going to take a miracle," Gina's mother murmured in disbelief. But she knew that she was talking to herself by now.

Having temporarily taken care of Sylvie's latest emergency and then checking on all the other recently handled pseudoemergencies to make sure that everything was progressing on schedule and that no new developments had taken place, Gina decided to reward herself and swing by Shane's house later that day.

Gina started talking the second that Shane opened the door. "I hope you don't mind my stopping by. But I was passing by this bookstore today and saw this big picture book in the window with that cartoon, *Happy Hound Puppies*, on the cover. I thought of Ellie because she said she liked watching that cartoon, so I got it for her." She indicated the shopping bag she had in her hand. "I hope that's okay," she added as an afterthought.

Shane took the bag from her. It felt heavy to him. "You did say one book, right?" he asked, looking into the shopping bag. "It looks like there are several in here."

Gina shrugged a little sheepishly. "Well, once I went into the store to buy that book, I saw a few others that I thought Ellie might like. I really couldn't make up my mind, so I bought all of them," she concluded with a smile.

Shane laughed at her explanation, touched that she was motivated to buy gifts for his niece. "I can see that."

Ellie had obviously heard Gina talking and came running in from another room to join Gina and her uncle. "Hi, Gina!" she cried. "We're having dinner. You can eat with us if you'd like. We have plenty—especially vegetables," she confided, lowering her voice when she came to the word *vegetables*.

Shane looked amused. "Ellie doesn't really like vegetables," he told Gina needlessly.

Ellie tossed her head, negating his statement. "I like mashed potatoes."

"You need green vegetables, munchkin," Shane reminded her.

Ellie pursed her lips in a frown. "My stomach can't see. It doesn't know the mashed potatoes aren't green," she informed her uncle.

Delighted by Ellie's spirit, Gina laughed. "Can't argue with that."

The next thing she knew, Ellie was grabbing her hand and pulling her toward the kitchen.

"Come to the table," she coaxed, echoing something she'd heard her uncle say to her.

Gina looked over her shoulder at Shane to see if this was all right with him.

Following behind them, Shane gestured toward the kitchen. "You heard the munchkin." He smiled at Ellie. "Come and eat with us."

She didn't need her arm twisted.

Gina stayed for dinner, which turned out to be pork loin. There were also two servings of vegetables, spinach and mashed potatoes. She saw Ellie deliberately avoiding the spinach on her plate.

"Did you know that if you mixed potatoes into the spinach, it doesn't taste like spinach at all?" Gina told Ellie. She proceeded to mix the two on her plate, then offered a small forkful to Ellie. "Try it," she coaxed.

Ellie made a face, then took the tiniest of bites, moving her head in and out like a small bird taking a drink of water.

"Not bad, eh?" Gina asked. "My mom used to do that to get me to eat my spinach."

"You didn't like green vegetables either?" Ellie asked, surprised and also pleased that she had something in common with Gina.

"Nope. Would you like some more?" Gina asked. She was aware that Shane was silently observing all this play out.

Ellie's head bobbed up and down. "Yes, please. It tastes like crunchy mashed potatoes."

Gina nodded, preparing the two vegetables for the little girl. "Good description."

After dinner, Ellie begged her to stay so that they could "read these books together."

"If it's okay with your uncle," Gina qualified, glancing toward Shane.

"Oh sure, he won't mind," Ellie confidently assured her. "He's a good guy."

Which was how Gina wound up helping Ellie read the books that she had brought over. Ellie insisted on reading all of them. Or at least most of them. Ellie's eyes began to droop by the time they had finished four books. By the middle of the fifth book, she finally lost her battle with her eyelids.

"You wore her out," Shane said. "Good job. It usually takes me a lot longer."

Moving aside the storybooks Ellie had surrounded herself with, Shane slipped one hand underneath his niece's body and slowly picked her up, taking care not to wake her up. Gina followed behind him as he carried the little girl up to her room.

"Want me to change her into her pj's?" Gina asked him.

"No, just take off her sneakers. If you start to change her out of her clothes into her pajamas, she might wake up and you would be amazed how recharged Ellie can get by taking a simple ten-minute nap."

"Taking off sneakers it is," Gina responded, slowly slipping off first one sneaker, then the other and placing them side by side at the foot of Ellie's bed.

Shane covered his niece with the princess throw she had at the edge of her bed, turned on her nightlight, then tiptoed out as he eased the door closed.

"You did that like a pro," Gina couldn't help telling him.

"I should. I've had more than three years of practice doing it." He stopped in the hallway and turned toward her. "With any luck, she's down for the night. What would you like to do now?" he asked Gina.

She knew that she should call it a night herself. She didn't want him to think she'd come here so they could pick up where they had left off the other night.

But for some reason, she couldn't seem to get her legs to work. Couldn't seem to make herself walk out unless he told her something that would make her feel she should go.

So rather than do what she felt was the right thing, Gina looked up at Shane and said, "Surprise me."

"I don't think," he told her, moving closer to her, slipping his fingers into her hair, "after the other night, that anything I did would surprise you."

She could feel his breath along her lips, feel anticipation instantly rising up, full of demands, within her veins.

"Why don't we test that theory?" she proposed.

He cupped her face in his hands as her heart continued to beat wildly in her chest. Her breath froze as he slowly lowered his mouth to hers. When he made contact, it felt like there were multicolored flares going off in her head.

Stifling a moan, Gina slipped her arms around his neck, rising up on her toes to further lose herself in his kiss.

After what felt like a blissful eternity, he released her and drew his head back.

"Too forward?" he teased.

"Just shut up and do it again," she told him.

Humor curved his lips. "If you insist," he said just before he kissed her again.

The kiss lasted longer this time, eroding what little there was left of her resistance. And when he drew his head away a second time, something inside of her almost let out a mournful cry.

"You know," he told her in a low, seductive voice, "if you're interested, my room's just down the hall. We'd have more privacy there, provided of course you want more privacy."

This would have been the perfect time to pretend that it didn't matter to her one way or another. A perfect time for her to play hard to get.

But she wasn't interested in playing any games. She was interested in soothing this ache that was building up inside of her, making wanton demands on her. If making herself available to Shane was the wrong way to play this, so be it. Despite the vocation she'd chosen that required her to hold jittery brides' hands, she wasn't versed in the games people played. She wanted there to be nothing but honesty between them because at bottom, honesty was all any of them had.

"Funny man," she quipped. "Take me to your lair," she told him.

His eyes were already caressing her. "I could carry you off," he offered. "Like Tarzan. Maybe even find a couple of trees to swing from."

"Just walk," she told him.

He grinned. "Yes, ma'am."

He took her hand in his and brought her into his bedroom.

The room all but reeked of masculinity with its sleek, straight lines. There was a framed portrait of a couple with two little boys on the bureau. She assumed that was a family photograph taken when he was a little boy. But other than that, and one framed photograph of Ellie, there were no other pictures, no other personal touches in the room.

She turned to ask him why the room was so devoid of other photographs of his family but found she couldn't. Shane had found something better for her mouth to do. And her heart rejoiced over it.

Chapter Eighteen

The wedding that Gina had seriously felt would never arrive finally did.

Her mother, bless her, had lived up to her reputation and had somehow brought the bride's semishredded veil back from the dead, although it had taken longer than anticipated.

Gina presented it to Sylvie just as the bride had finished getting into her sleeveless, floor-length wedding gown.

Carefully placing the veil on the bride's head, Gina kept her fingers crossed that Sylvie wouldn't notice that the veil was a little shorter than it had been before Cinnamon had gone to work on it.

"Oh, it's perfect," Sylvie cried with enthusiasm. "Thank you! I never would have been able to survive all this chaos without you."

She carefully looked herself over from every possible angle in the floor-length mirror. The mirror was set up in the chamber that had been set aside for the bride and her bridesmaids.

There was no hiding the pleasure throbbing in Sylvie's voice.

It was a quarter to one o'clock in the afternoon and the wedding in the newly repaired church would be starting in fifteen minutes. Gina herself had been up since six, working nonstop almost the entire time. She had been checking and double-checking a thousand and one details so that there were no unexpected surprises, otherwise known as emergencies, cropping up before the festivities had a chance to get underway.

They were almost at the finish line, Gina thought.

She would have liked to demur to Sylvie's comment about not being able to survive without her services, saying something to the effect that Sylvie was stronger than she'd thought and was up to handling whatever emergency came up. But that would have been an outright lie. Sylvie, Gina had come to realize over these last three weeks, was too high-strung to handle a hangnail, much less anything that was more stressful than that.

Not wanting to insult the woman on her big day, Gina merely replied, "That's what I'm here for, Sylvie." She smiled at the bride. "Glad I could help."

"I'm telling all my friends about you," Sylvie promised, looking herself over one last time. "Get ready to have your cell phone start ringing nonstop."

Gina merely smiled at the bride's comment. Most likely, once all this was over, Sylvie wouldn't remember this conversation.

The beginning strains of the wedding march wove

themselves into the room. "That's your cue," Gina told Sylvie. Turning toward the other bridesmaids, including the maid of honor, Gina asked, "Everybody ready? This is it." She turned back to look at Sylvie again. The latter suddenly began to look pale. "Sylvie, what's wrong?"

"I think I'm going to throw up," the bride wailed, pressing her hand to her stomach.

"No, you are not," Gina informed her in a stern voice, then, looking Sylvie in the eye, she instructed, "You're going to walk down that aisle on your father's arm and you are going to marry the man of your dreams. Do you understand?"

Sylvie acknowledged the question with the barest nod of her head.

"Yes," she said in a hoarse voice.

"All right then," Gina announced, placing one arm around the bride's waist, guiding the young woman through the door, "we all know our positions. Let's have a wedding!"

The five bridesmaids all filed out. Gina hung back until she could create a space for herself right in front of the maid of honor. Sylvie clutched at her one last time, mouthing the words "Thank you," before she released Gina's arm.

The music seemed to swell as Gina walked into the church directly in front of the maid of honor. Moving slowly, Gina kept her eyes focused on the altar. Even so, she still managed to do a quick scan of the immediate area.

She was looking for Shane.

According to her schedule, Shane and his assistant should have brought the wedding cake to where the reception was being held an hour ago. That would have given him plenty of time to set up the cake, then change into a formal suit and come to the church. Shane was her plus one.

Right after the ceremony was over and the photographs were taken, Gina intended to spend the rest of the reception with Shane.

Provided, of course, that he hadn't decided to leave after he had set up the wedding cake, she thought. She was beginning to suspect that might very well be a possibility as she came up to the altar and took her place with the other bridesmaids on the left side of the church.

Temporarily facing the congregation now, Gina quickly scanned the faces of the people waiting for the bride to reach the altar and her destiny.

Shane was nowhere to be seen.

Had he changed his mind after all? Gina struggled to contain her disappointment. She had to hold it together. This wasn't about her. This was Sylvie's day and she had to keep smiling for the bride's sake. The photographer was moving around, snapping pictures. Nobody needed or wanted a sad bridesmaid ruining the pictures.

If nothing else, she reminded herself, Sylvie had already paid her for her services.

Just as she was moving in closer to the right of the altar and the other bridesmaids, the sound of the outer door, the one leading into the church proper, caught her attention. Sparing one glance to the rear of the congregation, Gina thought she caught a glimpse of Shane. Her heart literally skipped a beat. He looked dashing, dressed in a dark suit.

She allowed herself one more look as the minister began the ceremony.

It *was* Shane.

He'd kept his word. The smile that took over her face was genuine this time.

As a relaxed sigh escaped her lips, she allowed herself to enjoy the wedding.

The photographer, Andre, a small nimble man with a sharp eye for composition, was extremely thorough and he seemed to be everywhere, almost at the same time. Although she was the one responsible for finding him and bringing the photographer to Sylvie, Gina began to think that Andre was never going to stop herding them from one spot to another, never stop issuing orders and snapping photographs.

By the time Andre was finally finished, Gina felt she was wilting. But it turned out that the photographer had just finished this part of it. He and his assistant were coming to the reception hall to continue preserving the wedding with his camera. In addition, a videographer named Suzanne was making sure she was preserving everything that happened at the reception on video, as well.

Despite all this going on, all Gina saw was Shane. The first moment she was able to, she made her way over to him, a broad welcoming smile on her lips.

"You made it," she cried.

"Barely," Shane answered. "The traffic getting here was an absolute bear," he told her. "Some driver decided that his SUV belonged in two lanes at once. Driving like he owned the road, it was only a matter of time before he caused a minor pileup. Luckily, it happened right in front of me."

Gina blinked. Had she missed something? "Luckily?" she questioned, stunned that Shane would phrase it that way.

"Well, if it had happened a mile ahead of me, I'd probably still be on the freeway, trying to get here. And, even luckier," he continued, "the guy missed me."

She smiled, shaking her head. "Leave it to you to bury the headline."

The band was playing a familiar slow dance. Shane leaned into her, a warm look in his eyes. "Dance with me?" he asked.

"I'm not all that good at dancing," she warned.

Gina wanted only to sit with him and just spend the time talking. Having him here had sunbeams bouncing around inside of her. Part of her had doubted that he'd actually show up. Granted they had made love several times in the last week, but that was a private thing. Dancing with him was far more of a public thing.

"C'mon, Gina," he coaxed. "All you have to do is sway from side to side. Nobody's grading you on this," Shane assured her as he took her into his arms. Just as he closed his arm around her, he drew back his head to look at her. "You're trembling. Are you cold?" he asked, although it didn't feel cool enough to warrant her reaction.

She shrugged off his question, then decided to be honest with him. "I was just thinking of you getting crushed by that SUV, that's all."

A smile played on his lips. "Well, if that had happened, there wouldn't have been a cake for the reception."

Gina closed her eyes, searching for strength. She banked down the urge to shout at him. "That's not what's important here," she told him, gritting her teeth.

Shane smiled at her. "No point in thinking about what might have happened, Gina. It didn't," he stressed, brushing the incident aside. Changing the subject, he

looked around as they continued dancing. "You put together a nice wedding."

While his compliment warmed her, she didn't feel
right about accepting it. "The wedding was already put
together when I took over. I just tweaked it in order to
get it on track."

"All right," he allowed, "you do a good job tweaking."
Shane's eyes crinkled as he grinned at her. "Although
it's a little too grand for my taste," he had to admit. "I
prefer something small and intimate." The look in his
eyes seemed to take her prisoner as he asked in a far
more seductive tone, "How about you?"

"Small and intimate is good," she agreed, the inside
of her mouth growing suddenly dry.

"You mean it?" he asked, surprised. "You'd be satisfied with a small church wedding? With just a few
friends and family members in attendance?"

"Yes," she answered, suddenly afraid to breathe because the next breath would undoubtedly dissolve the
dream she realized she was entertaining at this moment.
"Why?"

"Before I answer your question, I think we should
stop dancing," he prompted. When she looked at him
quizzically, he pointed out, "The music's stopped."

"Oh." She'd been so intent on listening to what Shane
was saying, she had managed to filter out everything
else. Including the band.

Embarrassed now, she moved from the small space
set aside for dancing and started to hurry back to her
table. She wanted the shelter provided by the guests who
were seated there. Shane couldn't laugh at her if there
were other people present—could he?

Shane caught up to her in a couple of strides. Taking hold of Gina's arm, he stopped her escape.

"Don't you want me to answer your question?" he asked.

Trapped, she relented. "All right. *Why* were you asking me if I'd be satisfied with a small wedding?"

"Because," he answered, "if you wouldn't be satisfied, then I'd opt to go with the whole package." He gestured around the large ballroom to get his point across. "With this," he specified. "Although it would mostly be up to you to fill it up."

"And we're back to 'why,'" she said. "Why would it be up to me to fill up a large room?" Her brain felt as if someone had shaken it like one of those snow globes. There were falling snowflakes all around her and nothing was clear. "Did you skip a step or did I miss something?"

She was utterly confused at this point. Moreover, she was really afraid to jump to a conclusion because she was afraid it would be the wrong one.

Shane took her further aside so that they were away from the other guests. "No, you didn't miss something. I'm the one who skipped a step." He took in a deep breath before continuing. "Mainly because I'm afraid that you'll shoot me down again if I ask."

Gina discovered that it was really difficult to talk with her heart in her throat, but somehow, she found a way. "I won't shoot you down," she promised, then whispered, "Ask."

It's now or never, he told himself. And with that, he started talking. "I have been in love with you for the last twelve years. Even after you laughed in my face and demolished my ego, I didn't stop loving you. I didn't want to love you," he admitted, "but there are some things that a person just doesn't have any control over." And loving her fell into the category.

"I didn't laugh in your face," she insisted. "That was just nervous laughter. I told you, I turned you down back then because I didn't want to get hurt."

"That still doesn't make any sense to me. I don't understand," he confessed.

Gina shook her head. "It doesn't matter. The only thing that matters is that I should have said yes then, the way I'm saying yes now—that is," she qualified nervously, "if you're seriously asking me to marry you now."

"Seriously, laughingly, I'll ask you any way you want me to, as long as your answer is yes," he told her. "I'm tired of missing you, Gina. Tired of regretting the life we should have had, but didn't. I don't want to waste any more time like that." He took her hands in his, looked into her eyes and quietly said, "Marry me, Gina."

"With my whole heart and soul, I want to say yes," she told him.

He caught the hesitation in her voice and the phrasing she had used. "But?"

Her response wasn't the one he expected.

"Did you tell Ellie about this? I'm not just marrying you, I'm marrying her, too. She belongs in this decision, Shane. What if she doesn't want you to get married?" she asked, clearly concerned.

Shane laughed with relief. "As a matter of fact, she gave me her blessing. Not in those exact words, of course, but I talked with her about this last night and she's very excited about the prospect of the three of us living together. She's got the whole thing planned out," he told Gina. "So, you see, if you turn me down, you'll also be disappointing Ellie because you'll be turning her down, too."

The wave of relief that flooded over her was unbelievable. "Then it's a good thing I won't be turning her down," Gina told him.

"So it's yes?" Shane asked her, wanting to be a thousand percent sure before he allowed himself to celebrate.

"It's yes." All of her was smiling now, inside and out. "Yes to both of you," Gina told him, wrapping her arms around his neck.

"That's good," he told her. "Ellie will be overjoyed."

She cocked her head as she looked up into his face. "And Ellie's uncle?"

He laughed. "That goes without saying," he said, about to lean in and kiss her.

But she drew her head back, trying to look serious, but not managing to quite pull it off. "Humor me, Ellie's uncle. Say it."

"Oh, I'll do better than that," he told her. "I'll show you."

And he did.

He showed her for a long, long time.

Epilogue

"I don't know how to thank you!" an elegantly attired Anna Bongino cried, throwing her arms around Maizie's neck. The floor-length silver mother-of-the-bride gown caught the light, shooting out bits and pieces of sparkling rainbows around the church. "You truly are a witch—the beautiful, good kind," Anna quickly clarified. She definitely didn't want to risk insulting her friend. "How did you ever manage it?" she asked. "How did you find Shane and bring them together?"

Celia smiled her pleased, mysterious smile. "Well, we could tell you, but then we'd have to kill you," she deadpanned.

"Don't pay attention to Celia," Theresa told Anna, waving a hand at her friend. "She's been watching way too many mystery thrillers on TV lately."

Glossing over Anna's question—they never liked

going into the details involved in their process—Maizie told her friend, "It's really very nice of you to have Gina invite us to the wedding."

"Nice?" Anna echoed. "Without you, there would *be* no wedding. I don't know how you did it, but I will be grateful and indebted to you until my dying day," she told the three women. "And whatever you need, whatever you want, all you have to do is ask."

Maizie's eyes shone as she smiled at her friend's enthusiasm. "We're just happy we could finally bring these two together."

"I hate to interrupt this, but I think we should find seats," Celia told the others. "I can see the organist getting ready to start playing."

Anna placed her hand over her heart, as if to ensure that it remained in her chest. She looked like a child on Christmas morning after being told that Santa Claus had been there, Maizie thought.

"It's happening," Anna cried excitedly. "It's really happening."

"Yes," Maizie replied with the pride of someone who had once again accomplished what she had set out to do, "it's really happening." Placing a hand on Anna's shoulder, she urged the woman, "You'd better take your seat up front."

Anna snapped to attention. "Oh right, of course. I'll see you all at the reception," she told the trio just as an usher approached her side, ready to escort her into the front pew.

"It isn't often we see a mother of the bride acting even more excited than the bride," Celia commented, amused, as she and her coconspirators filed into a pew on the bride's side of the church.

"I think it's kind of cute," Theresa said.

"Yes, it is," Celia agreed.

"Well, ladies," Maizie whispered to the others as all three sat down. "Mission accomplished. Again," she added with a twinkle in her eye.

Theresa chuckled. "Was there ever any doubt?"

Finally, Gina thought as she heard the organist begin to play the wedding march—*her* wedding march. After being a bridesmaid in so many weddings, it was finally her turn. She almost had to pinch herself.

It didn't seem real.

"Ready?" her brother-in-law asked, peering into the room.

Gina smiled at Eddie. Because her father had passed away several years ago, her sister's husband had volunteered to give her away.

"Ever so ready," she replied. Scooping up the ends of her veil, she walked out of the room, joining Eddie. "Thanks for doing this," she told him.

He carefully led her toward the inner doors of the church. "It's good practice for when I have to give Addie away," Eddie answered.

Gina wanted to run into the church to make sure that Shane was up there at the altar, waiting for her. But she forced herself to move slowly. And then they were in position, just behind the pint-size flower girl, ready to proceed to the altar.

Ellie turned around to flash a huge grin at Gina, then instantly adopted a very serious expression as she turned back around. Moving slowly with a surprising level of maturity, Ellie carefully scattered rose petals in front of her.

Shane's niece was out of petals by the time she reached the altar and it was clear she felt she had completed her job well. Winking at Gina, Ellie allowed herself to be led off to the side where the bridesmaids were gathered.

Gina's breath caught in her throat as she came to the end of her short journey. Her eyes met Shane's.

"You're on your own, Gee," Eddie told her affectionately, pausing to brush a quick kiss on her cheek.

Gina was barely aware of her brother-in-law or what he had just said. Every fiber of her being was totally focused on Shane.

Shane's smile was warm and welcoming. "You came," he whispered.

"Wild horses couldn't have kept me away," she answered just as the priest began to recite the time-honored words that would forever bind them together.

The warm, pleased smile on Shane's face burrowed into her heart.

This time, Gina thought, it was going to be all right. Finally.

She wanted to memorize ever single nuance and syllable of the ceremony, but the words the priest was reciting kept buzzing in and out of her head like bees filled with adrenaline. Gina found herself waiting to hear the ones that counted.

And then she did.

"I now pronounce you man and wife," Father Scanlon declared. Smiling, he told Shane, "You may kiss the bride."

Shane lifted up the veil from her face, the veil she had just discovered her mother had lovingly made for her ten years earlier in anticipation of her wedding.

"I've been waiting to kiss the bride for a long, long time," he told her just before he followed the priest's suggestion.

The kiss, they both thought, was well worth waiting for.

* * * * *

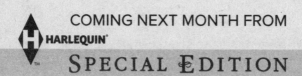

COMING NEXT MONTH FROM
HARLEQUIN®
SPECIAL EDITION

Available October 22, 2019

#2725 MAVERICK HOLIDAY MAGIC
Montana Mavericks: Six Brides for Six Brothers • by Teresa Southwick
Widowed rancher Hunter Crawford will do anything to make his daughter happy—even if it means hiring a live-in nanny he thinks he doesn't need. Merry Matthews quickly fills their house with cookies and Christmas spirit, leaving Hunter to wonder if he might be able to keep this kind of magic forever...

#2726 A WYOMING CHRISTMAS TO REMEMBER
The Wyoming Multiples • by Melissa Senate
Stricken with temporary amnesia, Maddie Wolfe can't remember a single thing about her life...or her husband, Sawyer. But even with electricity crackling between them, it turns out their fairy tale was careening toward disaster. Will a little Christmas spirit help Maddie find her memories—and the Wolfes find the spark again?

#2727 THE SCROOGE OF LOON LAKE
Small-Town Sweethearts • by Carrie Nichols
Former navy lieutenant Desmond "Des" Gallagher has only bad memories of Christmas from his childhood, so he hides away in the workshop of his barn during the holidays. But Natalie Pierce is determined to get his help to save her son's horse therapy program, and Des finds himself drawn to a woman he's not sure he can love the way she needs.

#2728 THEIR UNEXPECTED CHRISTMAS GIFT
The Stone Gap Inn • by Shirley Jump
When a baby shows up in the kitchen of a bed-and-breakfast, chef Nick Jackson helps the baby's aunt, Vivian Winthrop, create a makeshift family to give little Ellie a perfect Christmas. But playing family together might get more serious than either of them thought it could...

#2729 A DOWN-HOME SAVANNAH CHRISTMAS
The Savannah Sisters • by Nancy Robards Thompson
The odds of Ellie Clark falling for Daniel Quindlin are slim to none. First, she isn't home to stay. And second, Daniel caused Ellie's fiancé to leave her at the altar. Even if he had her best interests at heart, falling for her archnemesis just isn't natural. Well, neither is a white Christmas in Savannah...

#2730 HOLIDAY BY CANDLELIGHT
Sutter Creek, Montana • by Laurel Greer
Avalanche survivor Dr. Caleb Matsuda is intent on living a risk-free life. But planning a holiday party with free-spirited mountain rescuer Garnet James tempts the handsome doctor to take a chance on love.

**YOU CAN FIND MORE INFORMATION ON UPCOMING HARLEQUIN® TITLES,
FREE EXCERPTS AND MORE AT WWW.HARLEQUIN.COM.**

HSECNM1019

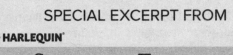
*Stricken with temporary amnesia, Maddie Wolfe can't
remember a single thing about her life...or her husband,
Sawyer. But even with electricity crackling between
them, it turns out their fairy tale was careening toward
disaster. Will a little Christmas spirit help Maddie find
her memories—and the Wolfes find the spark again?*

Read on for a sneak preview of
A Wyoming Christmas to Remember
by Melissa Senate,
the next book in the Wyoming Multiples miniseries.

"Three weeks?" she repeated. "I might not remember
anything about myself for three weeks?"

Dr. Addison gave her a reassuring smile. "Could be
sooner. But we'll run some tests, and based on how well
you're doing now, I don't see any reason why you can't
be discharged later today."

Discharged where? Where did she live?

With your husband, she reminded herself.

She bolted upright again, her gaze moving to Sawyer,
who pocketed his phone and came back over, sitting
down and taking her hand in both of his. "Do I—do we—
have children?" she asked him. She couldn't forget her
own children. She couldn't.

"No," he said, glancing away for a moment. "Your
parents and Jenna will be here in fifteen minutes," he

said. "They're ecstatic you're awake. I let them know you might not remember them straightaway."

"Jenna?" she asked.

"Your twin sister. You're very close. To your parents, too. Your family is incredible—very warm and loving."

That was good.

She took a deep breath and looked at her hand in his. Her left hand. She wasn't wearing a wedding ring. He wore one, though—a gold band. So where was hers?

"Why aren't I wearing a wedding ring?" she asked.

His expression changed on a dime. He looked at her, then down at his feet. Dark brown cowboy boots.

Uh-oh, she thought. *He doesn't want to tell me. What is that about?*

Two orderlies came in just then, and Dr. Addison let Maddie know it was time for her CT scan, and that by the time she was done, her family would probably be here.

"I'll be waiting right here," Sawyer said, gently cupping his hand to her cheek.

As the orderlies wheeled her toward the door, she realized she missed Sawyer—looking at him, talking to him, her hand in his, his hand on her face. That had to be a good sign, right?

Even if she wasn't wearing her ring.

SPECIAL EXCERPT FROM

HQN™

Seven years ago, Elizabeth Hamilton ran away from her family. Now she's back to end things permanently, only to discover how very much she wants to stay. Can the hurt of the past seven years be healed over the course of one Christmas season and bring the Hamiltons the gift of a new beginning?

Turn the page for a sneak peek at
New York Times *bestselling author RaeAnne Thayne's heartwarming Haven Point story*
Coming Home for Christmas, *available now!*

This was it.

Luke Hamilton waited outside the big rambling Victorian house in a little coastal town in Oregon, hands shoved into the pockets of his coat against the wet slap of air and the nerves churning through him.

Elizabeth was here. After all the years when he had been certain she was dead—that she had wandered into the mountains somewhere that cold day seven years earlier or she had somehow walked into the deep, unforgiving waters of Lake Haven—he was going to see her again.

Though he had been given months to wrap his head around the idea that his wife wasn't dead, that she was indeed living under another name in this town by the sea, it still didn't seem real.

How was he supposed to feel in this moment? He had no idea. He only knew he was filled with a crazy mix of anticipation, fear and the low fury that had been simmering inside him for months, since the moment FBI agent Elliot Bailey had produced a piece of paper with a name and an address.

Luke still couldn't quite believe she was in there—the wife he had not seen in seven years. The wife who had disappeared off

PHRTEXP1019R

the face of the earth, leaving plenty of people to speculate that he had somehow hurt her, even killed her.

For all those days and months and years, he had lived with the ghost of Elizabeth Sinclair and the love they had once shared.

He was never nervous, damn it. So why did his skin itch and his stomach seethe and his hands grip the cold metal of the porch railing as if his suddenly weak knees would give way and make him topple over if he let go?

A moment later, he sensed movement inside the foyer of the house. The woman he had spoken with when he had first pulled up to this address, the woman who had been hanging Christmas lights around the big charming home and who had looked at him with such suspicion and had not invited him to wait inside, opened the door. One hand was thrust into her coat pocket around a questionable-looking bulge.

She was either concealing a handgun or a Taser or pepper spray. Since he was not familiar with the woman, Luke couldn't begin to guess which. Her features had lost none of that alert wariness that told him she would do whatever necessary to protect Elizabeth.

He wanted to tell her he would never hurt his wife, but it was a refrain he had grown tired of repeating. Over the years, he had become inured to people's opinions on the matter. Let them think what the hell they wanted. He knew the truth.

"Where is she?" he demanded.

There was a long pause, like that tension-filled moment just before the gunfight in Old West movies. He wouldn't have been surprised if tumbleweeds suddenly blew down the street.

Then, from behind the first woman, another figure stepped out onto the porch, slim and blonde and…shockingly familiar.

He stared, stunned to his bones. It was her. Not Elizabeth. *Her*. He had seen this woman around his small Idaho town of Haven Point several times over the last few years, fleeting glimpses only out of the corner of his gaze at a baseball game or a school program.

The mystery woman.

Don't miss
Coming Home for Christmas *by RaeAnne Thayne,*
available wherever
HQN books and ebooks are sold!